Backlash

by

Karyn Good

Backlash

Contact Information: info@thewildrosepress.com

Cover Art by *Tina Lynn Stout*

The Wild Rose Press
PO Box 708
Adams Basin, NY 14410-0708
Visit us at www.thewildrosepress.com

Publishing History
First Crimson Rose Edition, 2012
Digital ISBN 978-1-61217-156-2
Print ISBN 978-1-61217-155-5

Published in the United States of America

"We have to work together, Chase."

Right. Against one of the most vicious gangs in the country. He caught sight of her pretty pink toenails peeking out from under her blanket. Him and the pretty little small town teacher up against Raphael Tessier. Maybe the bad guys would die laughing.

He meant to back away. To leave. Before her clean scent began absorbing into his skin. But with Lily, things never quite worked out the way he planned. Good intention turned into forward movement. Until they were chest-to-chest and hip-to-hip.

"Chase, be reasonable."

Reasonable? He could smell her. Her breasts pressed against his chest with every breath. He'd left reasonable so far behind he'd need a map to find it.

Then it was too late anyway. He needed to know if she tasted the same. Felt the same. And she was right there. In front of him. All he had to do was bend his head. Just a fraction of a movement and his self-imposed exile would end.

And he was only human.

So he tipped his head and put his mouth on hers. Ran the tip of his tongue over her bottom lip and got a yes to question number one.

His hands did a slow glide up her arms, over her shoulders to her face. He gently tilted her head and waited. Waited for the slight parting of her lips, the invitation to enter. When it came, it almost brought him to his knees.

He dove in like a man who'd been too long in the desert and she was his first taste of water in years. He needed his tongue in her mouth, tasting, savoring. He needed the warmth pulsing through his system to burn forever.

Dedication

For Jack, Always and Forever.

Chapter One

Lily Wheeler dug a pair of sunglasses out of the depths of her gigantic purse and plopped them on her nose. The back door of the school hissed shut behind her, leaving her smiling in anticipation. Seize the day. She repeated it over and over, keys clutched in her hand. As she started for her car, a huddle of young men in the middle of the lot snagged her attention. She paused. Something about the whole situation bothered her. Maybe their size? The way the small group was bunched together? She glanced at her watch. Bordering on late for her appointment, she wanted to dismiss it as nothing.

Still, weird to see the older students hanging out at this hour. She craned her neck to get a better view. Her teacher instincts tingled, but she strived to shrug them off. She didn't have time for more problems. A shortcut across the small patch of wilted grass led her straight into the parking lot. Her car sat in the far west corner, five yards past the knot of students.

At her approach, the tallest member of the group turned. She lifted her hand to wave, but her gesture fizzled in midair. Black ink sketched a spider web pattern up his neck and over his right cheek. Not pretty, not meant to be. He was no one she recognized. She tried to ignore the bony finger of fear scraping its way down her spine as ridiculous. This was Aspen Lake, not the big bad city.

Spider-Guy's lips moved, but the words drowned in the sea of space separating them. The rest of him remained stock still, arms crossed, legs braced until he shifted to stare past her and nod his head. Her internal alarm bells went from ringing to clanging. She didn't need to hear the heavy footsteps behind her to know someone was at her back.

The drama in front of her escalated. A vicious shove sent the man in the middle of the pack stumbling back. The push shocked her. She hesitated. All thoughts of her appointment with the real estate agent and the future went poof. She didn't know what they were trying to prove, but she couldn't ignore them any more than she could walk away. They were on school property. She had the ultimate say-so here, which was all well and good in theory.

She drew in a shallow breath. Time to take a stand. "No loitering. You're not supposed to be here. Move along." She hiked up the strap of her shoulder bag, tucked it against her, put a protective arm over it.

A second shove. It sent the victim, who was a good foot shorter than the rest, stumbling back and down onto the pavement. Sick recognition hit as she glimpsed the boy's face before he curled up into a ball. It shot the dynamics of the situation straight to worst-case-scenario.

"Enough. Leave him alone." She cleared the clog of fear out of her throat. The smirk of the man in front of her and the whisper of laughter from the one behind her stiffened her spine. No one messed with one of her students. Her students were her family. There was nothing she wouldn't do for family.

"Now," she demanded.

Another signal from the man facing her, and a cohort swung his boot into the ribs of the skinny boy huddled on the ground. Lily flinched, her stomach cartwheeling. The three men in front of her pivoted toward her with a creepy, military-like precision. Three pairs of dark eyes stared at her, not a twinge of apprehension on their unfamiliar faces.

Shocked silent, but not stupid, she slipped her hand into her purse and grabbed around for her cell phone. It's comforting shape found its way into her shaking hand. Her nerveless fingers wrapped around it. The wrenching pull on her shoulder made her gasp. The sight of her purse hitting the ground a good six feet away made her tighten her grip on the keys in her other hand. She carefully threaded them through her fingers.

"I dialed. So, you can leave peacefully, or you can stay and take your chances."

All three of the men crossed their arms and advanced. The move had an eerie, choreographed air to it. Like they'd done this before. Many times. Her vocal cords seized up. She swallowed, hoping to grease them loose.

"I mean it. You need to back off."

They laughed. She guessed redheads with curly hair, freckles, and wearing bubblegum pink capri pants didn't pass for intimidating. Her regular tactics might work with her younger students, but these weren't teenagers. This wasn't her classroom. This was an empty parking lot protected on one side by a six-foot high hedge of faded lilac bushes. A deserted street ran in front of the lot with a retirement home on the other side.

"Back. Away. Now." She planted her hands firmly on her hips, prayed it made her look taller and wider. Her keys dug into her skin, but she refused to wince or give anything away.

The gang leader's eyes hardened into little obsidian points. He raised his chin a notch. His lips peeled back from his teeth. In that second, the sun's rays dimmed, the temperature dipped, and the day got a whole lot darker.

The menace emanating from them wasn't feigned. It was shady, threatening, and it went bone deep. Lily stepped back, forgetting the man behind her until a large hand slapped against the space between her shoulder blades.

He pushed her forward. She drew in a discreet breath and shifted her weight, hoping to anchor her sandal-clad feet to the pavement. The sheen of fear-induced sweat coating her skin iced over as they closed in. The one with the ink shook his head slowly and tsked at her. Lily gritted her teeth.

When his booted feet came to rest toe-to-toe with her summer sandals, Lily didn't back down. She had no place to go. Heart hammering in her chest, eyes riveted on his cold face, she stood her ground. Needed to stand her ground for Jason's sake. She opened her mouth to scream. A grubby tattooed hand reached out to grab her chin and pull her closer. A lump of undiluted terror, not to mention revulsion, choked off her air supply. She refused to flinch when his grip tightened. She didn't dare breathe. She blinked past the telltale nausea. Managed to keep her lunch down.

"Listen up. This is none of your business." With his other hand, he drew the sunglasses down her nose, let them drop to the ground. He tilted his head, leaned in closer, and squeezed harder. Repelled, Lily tried in vain to pull back. He stopped an inch short of putting his lips on hers and whispered, "You saw nothing."

The sudden advent of squealing tires into the school's parking lot had Lily desperately trying to turn her head. Friend or more trouble? She caught a glimpse of a black truck before Spider-Guy yanked her head back. She clutched her keys, prepared to stab him in the stomach.

"Remember what I said." With a sneer and a

painful twist of his hand, her attacker released her. He glowered at the truck jerking to a halt and offered a hand signal to the others on the run. She didn't move, didn't breathe, didn't swallow, happy to be abandoned in favor of their exit strategy.

A man jumped out of the truck and yelled at the retreating men. The leader scrambled into their rusted out sedan, as smoke billowed from the spinning tires. She turned, stumbling toward the boy on the ground.

"Jason. It's okay, you're safe now." At least she hoped so. She still wasn't sure who was driving the truck. She dropped down beside the prone body and gently put her hand on her student's shoulder. Jason moaned as he rolled over.

"Is he okay?" A man hunkered down beside her.

"I don't know, yet. Jason, talk to me. Where are you hurt? No, don't move." She scanned his prone body without moving him. Offering all the support she dared by squeezing his shoulder.

"He needs to see a doctor. There's no sign of blood, but he took a vicious kick to the ribs." She turned to the man beside her, needing to explain, ready to unload at least part of the mental trauma of the last few minutes. But he had his cell phone pressed to his ear and his eyes trained on the direction taken by the retreating Buick. The line of his jaw made the hairs on her arms stand up. The dark wave of his hair triggered an image.

She froze.

He shut the phone, stuffing it back into his pocket. His weight shifted as he faced her, started to say something, and stopped. He stared, his outstretched hand never making it to Jason's shoulder. "Lily?"

She swallowed and then swallowed again because, holy crap, she hadn't hit her head had she? Was hallucinating a sign of trauma? Then her gaze locked with those oh-so-familiar blue eyes, and she knew.

Knew she wasn't hallucinating. Knew that, instead of a heap of crazy, she now had a mountain of insane. Chase Porter had disappeared from her life ten years ago. Had left town and left her, without a word, never to return. Until now. She'd had ten years to think of what she'd say to him if she ever saw him again. *Thanks for your help* had never crossed her mind.

"I'm okay. Really." Jason's voice yanked her back to the present. He attempted to get to his feet, pain contorting his young face.

"I've got him. Here, take it easy." Chase placed an arm around Jason's shoulders and slowly helped him to his feet. Maybe fear did cause some kind of twisted temporary insanity. Why else would she notice his build, the stretch of his leg, the lines of his face? Lines that hadn't been there ten years ago.

"What are you doing here?" she asked, because apparently stupidity was also a symptom of fear-induced insanity. Like his presence was the biggest thing she had to worry over. Like she cared that he had appeared out of thin air, in the nick of time, after disappearing for a decade.

"Rescuing you?" His hands settled on his hips. His eyes traveled the length of her and back up, right before he shook his head like he couldn't believe his bad luck.

Rescuing her? Was he kidding? One quick glance told her, no, he was one hundred percent serious. The black hair, the blue eyes, the height, it was all too familiar. The condescending attitude, that was new. And very unattractive.

"I had the situation under control, thank you very much." Disgusted, she shifted her focus to a more deserving subject, ignoring Chase's rude snort.

"How's your side?" She resisted the urge to

gather Jason up in a big hug. Instead, she searched for any signs of shock in his thin, pale face, noting the dilation of his pupils. His breathing, while shallow, didn't necessitate a call for an ambulance. She did, however, need to get him to a doctor.

Chase dug his cell phone out of his pocket, dialed, and paced out of her hearing range. She gulped in her first deep breath since leaving the school. He glanced back at them and she refused to look away. To give any indication his sudden return had upset her.

"I'm fine," Jason said as he braced his elbow against his side.

Lily gave herself a mental wake up call. "Come on, I'll help you into the school."

"No. I just..." Jason winced as he tried to take a deep breath. "I need to go home."

Lily sighed. "Jason, please, we need to check out your ribs. I can tell you're hurt." She put a hand on his shoulder.

"It's not bad, really. I can manage." Jason shrugged her hand off and sent a sulky scowl in Chase's direction.

Lily switched to plan B. "Okay, but I'll drive you." When he opened his mouth, she shook her head. "I will be taking you home and making sure you see a doctor."

"I think it would be better if I took you both to the police station," said Chase, coming up behind them.

She bristled at his tone, which made the words he'd uttered sound more like an order than an offer. It suited the new Chase to a tee. It did nothing for her blood pressure.

"Yes, of course. After he's seen a doctor." She forced her lips upward into an I-can-manage smile. She'd been managing for ten years without his assistance, without his touch or the sound of his voice, his laugh. No way was she getting into any vehicle, let alone that big black beast of a truck, with him.

"Dude, I'm not going anywhere with you." Jason crossed his arms and took a step closer to Lily.

Amen to that.

****

Constable Chase Porter shut his mouth before something stupid and irretrievable tumbled out. The words faltered over the tip of his tongue begging to be said, insane words like *please* or *beautiful* or worse yet, *forgive me*. His training saved him that humiliation at least. Bad enough to think the words, to have them clogging up his brain. He didn't need to open his mouth and spew his private longings into the open air. He swiped a sweaty hand over his mouth and regrouped. He couldn't afford distractions. Not now. Not when he was this close to Raphael Tessier and the Prairie Brotherhood.

And justice.

The piece of shit trash he'd come here to track down and lock up for a hundred years past forever had stood less then fifteen feet from him and gotten away. He should be furious. Needed to be furious. Anything other than twisted up and frantic. Tessier had touched her. Threatened her. The thought made his lunch turn to slop. In the interest of staying sane, he shoved all those thoughts back.

He needed to get her and the boy out of here. "Look, I can take you where you need to go. It's probably safer that way."

Her hand went to her throat, her lethal blue eyes widened, and the cornered animal look returned. "Safer? You don't think they'll come back?"

"No, but I don't want to take any chances. How bad is he hurt?" He eyed the kid, estimated his height to be approximately five feet, skinny, with stringy dark hair hiding most of his face. The Prairie

Brotherhood's newest gang member? A recruit?

"His name is Jason." She glanced at the stone statue of a kid standing next to her. "I'm not sure how bad it is. He definitely needs to see a doctor."

Jason didn't seem to agree. He started to shake his head, then winced and stopped.

Lily placed a hand on the kid's arm and leaned in to say something Chase didn't catch, then handed him her keys. She waited while Jason slouched his way toward a little red Volkswagen before turning back.

"Thanks for the help, but I can handle it from here." Her chin lifted, and her shoulders went back as she faced him down. He couldn't help but be impressed. Other than a little shaky around the edges, she was holding it together. Then again, she had no idea who she'd come up against.

"He needs to come down to the police station." His stating the obvious caused her chin to elevate another notch.

"I'll make sure things get done." The implication was clear. She'd do it without any help from him. He'd been dismissed. "Don't worry. We'll both be there."

"I'm not suggesting you won't. All I'm suggesting is that sooner rather than later would be better. While details are fresh in his memory." He dialed it back, trying to get a handle on his out of control emotions. For the first time since becoming a cop, he struggled to find his professional rhythm.

His hands clenched into fists as she walked away. It left him no choice but to trail after her like a lost puppy. She scooped up her purse, gathered its contents, and slung the strap over her shoulder. Next, she rescued her sunglasses and stuffed them inside, all while ignoring his existence.

"Are you sure you're all right?" Professional conduct required him to ask, memories begged him to double check and triple check. To reach out a hand.

She snorted. "Yes. Thanks so much for asking. I'm fine. We're all fine." She hugged her giant purse closer, and he frowned.

Her freckles stood out in stark relief against the pale canvas of her skin. The same freckles he'd played connect the dots with all those years ago, before he married his job. That same index finger twitched with the memory. Memories buried under a career, other women, and a promise.

He nodded at her purse. "Do you have a cell phone in there?"

"Yes. I do. Not that it's any of your business."

Oh, how he wished.

"Good," he said. "I doubt you'll need it, but keep it handy just in case." He glanced at his watch. "I'll meet you at the police station in half an hour."

He didn't give her time to protest. Didn't stop to explain. Didn't allow himself time to change his mind or regret his rudeness. He headed for his truck and sanity. Time to concentrate on the bad guys. On what he did best. Raphael Tessier was on his turf now. It may have been a few years since he covered the ground hereabouts, but some details never left you no matter how hard you tried to forget them. All he needed to do was line RT up in his sights and close the deal.

****

Typical.

Over, she reminded herself, and behind her. Way behind her. Swampy, muddy water-under-the-bridge behind her. She opened her mouth to debate the highhandedness of his plan, but his long legs were already putting distance between them while hers were wobbling again.

What had just happened here?

A random attack against a student? Not so

random? And what was with Chase Porter showing up in the nick of time, like they were pantomiming some warped white knight fairy tale? Except the players had been flesh and blood real. At least the walking away part was in character. Déjà vu anyone?

But Jason? He was thirteen. She'd bet her down payment the ringleader was in his mid-twenties. His eyes had had a century lived in hell look to them. What was his connection to Jason? She repressed a shudder at the possibilities and headed for her car. They needed to get the heck out of here before the sky starting falling.

Climbing in, she glanced at Jason, who was wedged up against the passenger door, staring out the window with mutinous zeal. She read his body language loud and clear——don't talk to me and don't notice me. She ignored it.

"Do you want to tell me about it?"

"No."

Of course, he didn't. Could there be anything more humiliating? She tried again. "Who were they?"

"Don't know."

She navigated her way around a corner. Took another stab at getting him to open up. "Do they know you?"

A shrug.

"What did they say to you?"

"Nothing."

"They must have said something."

"Nothing." He swiped at his cheek, and her heart squeezed. "They didn't say anything."

Uh huh, right. "Did you say something to them?"

"No."

"And you didn't recognize any of them?" He shifted to close the last half a millimeter gap left between him and the door, then shook his head.

Lily braked in front of a rundown, shabby bungalow and sighed at the sight of the black four-by-four pulling out to drive past. She hadn't noticed Chase behind her. Hadn't thought to look for him. Or anyone else, for that matter.

Was it a bad thing to yearn for a drink? Or several drinks?

Especially considering she was now required to leave Jason in the care of his sure-to-be-drunk father and trust him to get Jason the help he needed. Yeah, not likely.

She wished she could take him home, feed him soup and sweet tea. Pamper him a bit, even though she knew Jason would hate it. Thirteen-year-olds had their pride. And sure enough, the second her car rolled to a stop, Jason reached for the door handle.

"Wait a minute," she said. Jason groaned and waited. "Instead of having you come down to the station, I'm going to go talk to the police. I'll let them know where you are, so they can find you if they have any questions. I also have to report this incident to the principal." She held up a hand, forestalling any comment. "I have no choice, Jason. What would have happened if I hadn't come along when I did? If you don't want to talk to me, consider going to talk to Constable Mike. Okay?"

"Fine." He climbed out of the car and slammed the door shut. When she got out as well, he glared at her. "What are you doing?"

"I'm coming in to talk to your father."

"He's not here."

"I can't leave you here alone, Jason. You need to see a doctor." His slender form sagged as he clenched his fists. Not for the first time, she wished she could fix things for him. To give him the home and family he deserved, a place with laughter and love and food on the table, a place to thrive.

"My aunt lives down the street. I'll go there."

"Fine with me. Get in."

"What? It's like just down the street. I can walk."

"Or I could drive you." She walked around to his side of the car and opened the door.

Sullen silence filled the vehicle on the drive to his aunt's. She walked him to the door despite further protests. She explained the situation to his elderly aunt, and when she left, the phone book was out on the table with the doctor's number circled and an appointment booked. Cookie crumbs and an empty milk glass rested at Jason's elbow. Sometimes, a bit of well-deserved fussing worked better than a prescription. It would do him a world of good. She knew it did her a world of good to see it.

Lily climbed in behind the wheel and sucked in a deep breath. Next stop, police station. Right after she got the shaking part under control. She lifted a hand to her jaw and rubbed at the bruised skin. She pulled down the sun visor in front of her to check the tiny mirror, then slapped it shut. She didn't have time to work a cosmetic miracle. A glance at her watch showed her she was already seven minutes late. She shoved the keys in the ignition. Time for some answers.

Chapter Two

Chase rubbed at the grinding ache settling in at the base of his skull. Gang violence showing up in the tranquility capital of the world proved what law enforcement knew for a fact: gang activity was escalating in both rural and urban districts. The infestation extended across the country. Controlling it was like trying to shovel a hill of shit with a teaspoon. Raphael Tessier seldom left the cover of his hill. His appearance in Aspen Lake was an anomaly. Chase needed to know what had necessitated the out of character move. And what did a scrawny teenage boy have to do with any of it? Or his teacher?

He paused in the open doorway and studied the five feet, four inches of complication seated at the battered metal table. His jaw clenched as Lily tucked a strawberry blond curl behind her ear. After a span of ten years, the girl-next-door look she had going on still had the power to muddle his brain. Instead of focusing on the bad guys, every taste bud he owned was salivating—each fingertip was coveting a touch.

It was bloody demoralizing.

Fantasizing didn't have any place in his game plan. He needed to strategize. He had zero time for small town, freckle-faced schoolteachers who smelled like blue sky, wheat fields, and the toughest decision he'd ever made. He cleared his throat and pushed away from the doorframe. Time to put his money where his mouth was.

"Lily."

She flinched at the sound of her name. He gestured to a chair across from her, waited for her nod of permission. And because he'd morphed into a pathetic loser, he noted the slow slide of her tongue over her bottom lip, the skittish eye movements, along with the infinitesimal head bob. He tossed the file he'd been holding onto the table between them. The slap of sound calmed his nerves as he settled into the chair.

"Can I get you anything?" *Coffee, tea, protective bubble wrap.*

She lifted up the disposable cup in front of her. "No, thank you."

"Where's Jason?" He shifted on the hard seat. "Is he all right?"

"He's on his way to the doctor's."

"Okay. Then what can you tell me about the confrontation in the parking lot?"

"Shouldn't we wait for one of the officers before getting into that?"

"Right now, I'm it."

"I don't understand." Her fingers tightened around her cup, and the resulting pop from the pressure filled the small space. She glanced back at the door, all confusion, and he knew she was hoping for some kind of intervention. For someone else to join them, anyone else. "What do you have to do with all this? Why are you back here?"

Stalling, he settled his arms on the tabletop. She didn't trust him. He also got that he was the last person she'd want dropping back into her life. The file between them held some of her answers. The rest were buried so deep inside him, it made ignoring them all part of the routine.

He offered her an anemic look of confusion.

"Here?"

"Yes. Here. In this room. In Aspen Lake. In the parking lot of my school." She spread her hands out and motioned around her. "Here!" She averted her gaze and inhaled a deep breath before spotlighting him, apprehension darkening her eyes, deepening the blue color.

"My job." To him, it was that simple.

"Your job?"

"I've been transferred to the Aspen Lake detachment."

"You're a cop?" Her look of skepticism said it all. The air of disbelief pricked at his ego. He shifted in his chair. Like all the times in fifth grade when his teacher, Miss Carlisle, had asked him why he had no lunch. Had asked questions about his father.

"Is that so hard to believe?" He had worked his ass off to get where he was, and he was a damned good cop. The work he did with the Combined Forces Special Enforcement Unit, and his reputation, proved his dedication to his job. None of which she'd be aware of, or care about if she did. When he burnt a bridge, the only thing he left behind was ash.

"Yeah, kind of. But then, how would I know? You didn't feel the need to let me in on all your plans. Remember."

"So, we're going to do that here? Now? Rehash the past?"

"You're right. There's absolutely no need. Feel free to skip ahead to the part about why you're back now."

"Among other things, I'm part of a collective task force targeting organized crime."

"Which doesn't explain why you're back in Aspen Lake."

"Doesn't it."

She crossed her arms. "You think we have organized crime in Aspen Lake?"

While it had never been his, he needed to remember this was her place, her town, and her sanctuary, as well as a police matter. He kept his response brief. "Yes."

"And the attack this afternoon? You think it was gang related?"

"And you don't?"

She didn't react, didn't deny, which told him a lot.

He sighed. "We know gangs are recruiting in the area. One gang in particular is increasing its presence, the Prairie Brotherhood. They run the gamut from drugs to money laundering and everything in between."

"What's any of this got to do with Jason? He's a thirteen-year-old child."

"That would be the question of the hour. Because one of the men who attacked him this afternoon, the one with the web tattoo, is a prominent member of the Prairie Brotherhood."

She frowned as she uncrossed her arms and leaned forward. "But that doesn't make sense."

"Why?" He asked, because he needed all the facts, all the information on Jason he was able to gather, and figured his best bet was sitting in front of him.

"Because it just doesn't."

"You're going to have to be a little more specific."

"How would Jason even know this person?"

He tapped a finger on the file folder between them. "This person goes by the name Raphael Tessier. On the street he's known as the Enforcer, that's also his job description, by the way, and he's the number three man for the Prairie Brotherhood."

Her palms settled on the table, and her chest expanded with the long slow exaggerated breath she drew into her lungs. "But what could he want with Jason? I can't imagine Jason knowing this Enforcer person."

"Or how the Enforcer knows him?"

"No." She shook her head. "No idea."

"How well do you know Jason?"

"Well enough to know he'd never get mixed up in this kind of thing."

"Then apparently you don't know him as well as you think. The Prairie Brotherhood doesn't send out Raphael Tessier to terrorize kids. He has foot soldiers for that. He comes out when there's a very heavy score to settle. When all other options have failed. When only the most brutal tactics will do."

Hard to believe her skin could get any paler, but it did. He squelched the wave of pity and braced his arms on the table, ready to push back his chair. He needed distance. She reached across the table and laid a restraining hand on his arm. Before he knew it, memories got the drop on him. Of their special spot, of fogged over windows, of fumbling fingers and stubborn buttons. He set his butt back down in the chair. He didn't have a choice. Standing wasn't an option.

"So, you think..." She paused, collected herself. "You think they'll be back. Looking for him again. Don't you?"

He glanced down at her hand, registered the burn of his skin underneath hers. A four second time delay occurred before he stabilized enough to reply. "That's what we have to find out."

Her eyes squeezed shut for a couple of seconds. Her fingernails cut into his arm. "All right, you say you know your stuff. Tell me how to help him. I can talk to him. I can help."

He carefully and methodically removed her hand from his arm and placed it on the table. "You can let the police do their job."

She blinked, and the faintest flush of pink painted her throat and cheeks. "I need to do—"

"No, you don't." He gritted his teeth as she tucked her hands into her lap.

Her chin went up. "I'm involved whether you like it or not, so let's skip past all the crap and move on to what I can do to help him. Because the one thing I will not do is stand aside and leave him to be terrorized by these...these people."

Damn right you will, he thought. "Let's not pretty it up. These people? These people are killers, thieves, drug dealers, and pimps. The police will handle it. The police will keep him safe." He knew what happened to the people caught in the Prairie Brotherhood's headlights, and she was the very last person he wanted trapped there.

"No offense, but from everything you've said, it might not be enough." A true teacher, she held up a hand as soon as he opened his mouth. "He is in my classroom five days a week. I can help keep him safe. You can concentrate on the bad guys and put every effort into finding them. I, on the other hand, will be concentrating on my student." She let her hand drop, took aim and fired her parting shot. "He's all alone. His father couldn't care less. You, of all people, should be able to relate."

He closed his eyes at the low blow. Then he moved, made his way around the corner of the table, and came to stand beside her chair. "Still collecting lost souls, Lily?"

Her top teeth snagged on her bottom lip, and heat swept under his skin. She pushed her chair back and stood. "I don't need to justify my actions to you."

"You will if those actions put you, or anyone else, in danger."

"You seem pretty sure of yourself." Her hands went to her hips. "That's new."

"I do what it takes to get the job done." No matter what.

"And when the job's done? When there's nothing left for you here? Then you're gone?"

He deserved the demand. Didn't like it, but deserved it. He shoved his hands in his pockets, anything not to reach out. He stared down into the face that had played a part in every wet dream and nightmare he'd ever had. He forced his head back into the game and wished it was as simple as leaving the second he'd apprehended Tessier. "I'm not here to get in your way. Or make things more complicated than they need to be, but..." Since he was on a roll, he figured he might as well spill the rest of the good news. "Having said all that, you should know I've rented the old Hartford place."

"The Hartford place? But that's..."

"I know, next door to you."

It had been the only place available on short notice. He figured somewhere, high above the clouds, a very fickle deity was rolling on the floor laughing.

****

My house.

She blinked.

Number 72 Souris Street was supposed to be her house. Not someone else's house. And definitely not *his* house. *Her* house. The one she'd been on her way to put a down payment on before some whack job gang banger had interrupted her.

She needed to sit down.

Pride kept her standing, but didn't stop the flush of anger or the chaser of fear. Big time gang members were terrorizing one of her students. Chase Porter was moving in next-door, only a hedge and a poplar tree away. Her brain was going to need disaster relief.

"Lily?"

She wrapped her arms around her favorite purse. "I have to go." Before the sky fell or pigs flew past the window. She locked her sights on the door and escape.

"Why don't you let me take you home?" A worried tone crept into his superior attitude.

She started to laugh, then stopped. "No."

"I think—"

"No." She lifted a hand and headed for the door. "I'm fine." She couldn't seem to catch her breath, and her right eye was beginning to twitch, but otherwise, she was fine. If she left. Now.

She walked out and made it through the main doors. Then across the parking lot into her car. All without screaming, which did wonders for her hanging-by-a-thread sanity.

Autopilot got her home. Back in her tiny bungalow, she headed for her Lilliputian sized office. Flopping into her chair, she concentrated on her breathing. One deep cleansing breath at a time until she worked her way toward a complete yoga breath. A sense of calm settled over her. She kept her eyes closed for a few seconds longer. Once they were open, she placed a hand over the little ornamental box resting on her desk, picked it up, and held it over the garbage can. Her fingers refused to let it go. Disgusted, she opened a drawer and shoved it all the way to the back.

She brought up her favorite search engine. Settling in, she rotated her shoulders, kicked off her sandals, and placed her fingers on the keyboard. Research time. She put everything else out of her head. Knowledge was power, and she had every intention of arming herself to the teeth.

Once upon a time, she'd trusted Chase Porter with everything. He'd destroyed that trust. She wasn't giving it away again.

****

Lily rolled her eyes at the plate of freshly baked muffins in her hand. Okay, maybe not her best idea, but she was determined to follow through with it.

She stuffed the file folder she'd labeled *Probable Theories/JMcC* into her purse and pulled her front door shut behind her.

At five in the morning, dropping in on Chase on her way to school had made perfect sense. They had theories to discuss. Besides, it was a small town, there were new neighbor rules to adhere to and follow. One of them involved not showing up empty-handed, lame as that might sound to an outsider.

She planned on a friendly, but not too friendly, faintly interested, but not too interested, I-couldn't-care-less-about-you approach to getting her point across. He needed her help with Jason. She was rational, intelligent, and enlightened. He was smug, arrogant, and unreasonable. How hard could it be to outwit him?

She stowed her purse in her car, put one foot in front of the other making her way down the silent street. Picked her way over the crumbling walk and up the broken steps of the verandah to the chirping of songbirds. She smoothed her free hand down over the front of the pretty leaf green sundress she'd selected. With a "neighborly" smile pasted on, she knocked. And waited. And knocked again. Nothing.

Frowning, she glanced back over her shoulder to make sure she hadn't conjured up the huge black four-by-four in the driveway. Nope, still there. She leaned in to listen for movement, heard nothing, and knocked louder. She winced as she shook out her stinging knuckles.

Where could he be? Out serving and protecting? On foot? More likely he was busy defacing the original plaster walls, ruining the vintage paneling or scratching the finish on the antique claw-foot tub. Wait until she got a hold of her weasel of a real estate agent.

Add to that, she stood loitering on Chase's front steps, baking in hand, for all her...their neighbors to see. The neighbors of their very small town. She eyed the window a few feet down the porch, glanced down the empty street, past the construction sized garbage bins across the way blocking her view, then back at the large front window, figuring it was worth the risk. She shuffled down a few steps and squinted at the dirty windowpane, trying to see past the layers of grim.

"Darn it," she muttered as she pressed a little closer. "Where is he?"

"Looking for me?"

Letting out a squeak, Lily swung around and, to her horror, sent muffins spilling in all directions across the wide front porch. She bent to retrieve as many of the dancing muffins as possible and collided with Chase, intent on doing the same.

"Oh." She fell back on her butt, one hand on the file folder tucked under her arm and one balancing the plate of remaining muffins.

"Sorry about that." He offered a hand as he straightened up. "Here, let me help you up."

She gave him the plate, then without thinking, she put her hand in his other one and let him pull her up. Tactical error. She landed way too close. The man was a furnace. Heat radiated off him in waves. Too embarrassed to meet his eyes, she focused on his neck and discovered a fascinating little drop of water making its way down his throat, followed by another, and another. A glance up. The drops were dripping off his wet hair. Her eyes went down, tracked the drops as they mingled with the ones skimming over wide shoulders, down his very naked chest, and lower.

Sweet Mercy.

He'd managed to zip up his jeans, but not button the waistband, which hung open, the little gap in denim playing havoc with her equilibrium. She yanked her hand out of his and backed up, wiping it down the side of her dress.

Stop staring.

Staring was rude and bad for her mental health.

"I didn't hear you." He grimaced as he brushed a hand over his wet chest and then dried it off on his jeans. "I was in the shower."

So not the mental picture she needed at the moment. Not when her libido had the equivalent of an ice cream headache—too much, too fast. The last thing she needed was another tasty psychological lick.

"Thanks." He eyed the battered muffins. "I appreciate it."

"It's a welcome to the neighborhood and a thank you for your help yesterday…thing." She cleared her throat and forced herself to focus. "Do you have a minute? I have some questions and some things I'd like to run by you."

"Sure. What's up?" Before she realized his intention, he reached out and tucked a strand of hair behind her ear. The familiar gesture drove them both back a step. He shoved his hands in his jean pockets. It widened the gap in his waistband a little further. Not that she noticed. Not on purpose, anyways. Although the whole situation did have a certain train jumping the tracks feel.

A jaw muscle jumped as he cleared his throat. "About yesterday. This kid, Jason, could be in real trouble."

His zipper was starting to show signs of strain, like her nerves. *Focus.* "That's why I needed to talk to you. I have a couple of theories."

"Theories?" Confusion deepened the lines of his forehead.

"Yes, I did some research last night."

"Research?" She might have imagined the narrowing of his eyes, but she didn't think so.

"On the computer. And I think—"

"Wait a minute. Research on what?" His hands exited his pockets and settled on his waist.

Was he having trouble keeping up? "On gangs, gang culture, everything to do with gangs."

"Why?" The warm toasty feeling of a minute ago frosted over.

She stared at him. "Because, clearly, there are things I need to know as I'm in the middle of dealing with the fallout of gang activity."

"The police will handle it." Each word came out on a fierce puff of breath.

"Of course," she backtracked. She benefited from a deep breath and continued, "But I can help."

"How? How can you help?" His brows shot up. He paused, considered, showed some teeth, and then lifted a finger. "Now that I think of it, you can help. You can stay out of my way. Because the last thing I need is some Mary Poppins do-gooder type screwing up my investigation and waving her version of an umbrella like a red flag in Raphael Tessier's face."

"Mary Poppins? Do-gooder?" Lily clamped her mouth shut. For all of ten seconds. He'd actually had the audacity to point a finger at her. Her! She stuck out her own finger. "How dare you. And if you think I'm leaving Jason's safety in your hands, you have another think coming. You don't tell me what to do."

"I can and I will." Chase shrugged. "A badge gives me the right." He continued before she had a chance to interrupt. "So, do the police a favor, and don't interfere."

"I am in this whether you like it or not. And at the risk of repeating myself, I don't take orders from you."

"Jason is in over his head, and so are you if you think these are reasonable people. This is a criminal organization, people who specialize in intimidation, and they'll do anything to get what they want. Anything. By now, they've already got your name, your address, all they need to know."

Lily shook her and said, "Good thing I don't have anything they want."

Chase gaped at her. "You stand for the boy. You stand in their way. That is not a place you want to be, trust me."

He had to be kidding. Trust him? "Better to leave him standing there alone? I can't, and I won't, do that. He hasn't got anybody else. And the last person I'd trust on the face of this planet is you."

He swiped a hand through his hair and huffed out a breath. "He won't be alone, Lily. We'll be there to protect him. If you want to help, find out what they want with him and pass on the information to the authorities. Don't make the mistake of dragging the past into this."

"I can't ignore what's happened, and I'm not walking away from this situation, no matter how ugly it gets."

Chase let out a short, humorless laugh. "How about listening to reason?" He put out a hand. "No one is suggesting you don't support him. I'm saying leave it there, let the professionals deal with the criminal aspect of it."

"What is it you think I'm going to do? Search out gang members all on my own? I'm not stupid."

"I didn't say you were, but I also don't want to see you get hurt." And he said it all with a straight face. Like he cared. About her. Color her unimpressed.

She couldn't help it, she laughed. "I can look after myself, thanks." Hurt? It hurt standing here. On what was supposed to be her front porch with the man who'd ditched her for the bright lights of the big city two seconds after she'd given him everything. "I'll be fine. With or without your help." She set a foot down on the first step.

"You need to leave it alone, Lily." The warning

echoed in her ears.

She turned back. "Don't worry, I've got all sorts of tricks stashed in my carpetbag and I'll have you know, I happen to be very handy with an umbrella. In fact, I know just the place I'd like to shove it." With a parting glare and an exit worthy of a Broadway actress, including a perfect flounce, she left him standing on his droopy front porch. He could Mary Poppins that!

Chapter Three

Was it too much to ask for a reasonable attitude? Her fingers tightened on the steering wheel. Instead, she got overbearing, domineering, and pushy. The jerk.

And what was with the Mary Poppins reference? So now it was a crime to assist people, help each other out? He needed a refresher course on small town philosophy. She did have a brain in her head, after all. One that worked. You'd think someone returning after a lengthy absence would appreciate her input. Not Chase Porter. Fine. Let him labor under the mistaken impression he knew everything.

She whipped her cherry red Volkswagen Beetle into her usual spot. As of this moment, she was done obsessing over Chase Porter. No more attention given to gleaming wet abs, muscles, or bumps of any kind. Anatomy class was over. Jason faced very real, very serious problems. The whole town did. She jabbed the seatbelt release button and waited for the seatbelt to snap back.

A shiver shimmied up her spine as she scrutinized the parking lot. Cars, trucks, and one mint condition Harley Davidson motorcycle occupied yesterday's empty spaces. Normal colored the whole lot. She tugged the edges of her lightweight summer sweater closer together.

She climbed out of her vehicle and paused beside it. The scene didn't look different, didn't smell different, and it didn't sound different, not on the surface. But beneath the normal, an ugly undertone, absent prior to yesterday, drew breath and exhaled a cloud of menace over the school.

And Jason.

The Prairie Brotherhood's presence more than worried her, and the idea of a man like Raphael Tessier scared the stuffing out of her. The thought of Jason turning to these people to fulfill a need for family terrified and shamed her. Article after article suggested thirteen as a vulnerable age for at-risk youth like Jason, ignored, impoverished——invisible. On the surface, gangs promised at-risk children a place to belong, a sense of family, nourishment. They gave them colors, an identity. In return, the kids stole cars, beat their best friend bloody, pimped out their little sister, and worse.

Not happening. Not here. Not to her student. Or any student. He was no longer invisible. He had her whether he or Chase liked it or not. Gangs may look out for their own, but they had nothing on her or this town. She ran a hand over her hair and straightened her dress and sweater. She and this town had done a crappy job so far, but they would see who looked after who best in the end.

First item on her agenda? Report incident to the principal. Mental shudder. The thought of enlisting Amanda Henry's aid caused a brain bashing drum solo to start knocking around in her head. In the time it took to cross the parking lot and get to the principal's office, it segued into a skull splitting heavy metal concert. She stuck her head in the doorway and winced at the school secretary.

"Hi, Lora. She in?"

The school secretary offered a brief eye roll before nodding. "She is."

Aspen Lake's high school principal was as approachable and sympathetic as a budget report and as prickly as a porcupine. Thankfully, she was a gray streak and bone rattle away from retirement, which couldn't come soon enough for the entire faculty and staff.

She eyed the closed door to the principal's office. "That bad?"

"One too many teachers making requests for, and I quote: 'unreasonable and unnecessary foolery.'" She huffed out a sigh. "Gonna take your chances?"

"No choice."

The secretary shrugged. "I'll let her know you're here."

By the time she finished her accounting of yesterday's attack, Amanda Henry was frowning, and Lily was experiencing the symptoms of a brain aneurysm.

Ms. Henry tapped a pencil on her desk. "Are you sure you're not overreacting?"

Valid question. Because she did that all the time. Overreacted over little things. She bit down on her tongue. "I know what I saw."

"I mean, the idea of gangs? Here? Seems pretty farfetched to me."

Not according to her new font of information on everything gang related. She quirked a brow. "The police officer looking into the incident doesn't seem to think so."

"Which police officer? Constable Davenport?"

"No, this officer is fairly new to the detachment." *Although you probably remember him, in ninth grade he super glued every drawer of your desk shut, including the one hiding your bulletproof brand of hairspray and stash of travel magazines.* She coughed and covered her mouth to hide a reluctant smile.

"Well, there you go. He's likely overreacting, too. Trying to build something out of nothing and make a good impression on his new colleagues." She waved a hand in the air. "Doesn't understand how small towns work." She picked up a piece of paper from her desk. "Talk to Mike, he'll set him straight."

"With all due respect, I don't think that's the case." But she might have saved her breath for all the notice her words received.

Without bothering to look at her Ms. Henry continued, "And please remind Jason of the very real consequences for fighting on school property." She reached for another paper. "Now if you'll excuse me, I have to get to the announcements and then to a budget meeting where I will waste still more breath in a futile attempt to get the board to allot us another teacher." She pointed a finger. "Talk to Mike, get this straightened out."

Lily hoisted herself out of her chair. Mission accomplished.

Ms. Henry picked up another piece of paper then thwacked the whole bunch back down on her desk. She dipped her head to peer over the top of her half-moon glasses. "And Lily? Don't go making mountains out of molehills."

She bit her tongue halfway off. Reminded herself not to quibble. She'd gotten what she came for. Her boss's blessing to go to Mike for help with Jason. Her headache eased a fraction. Constable Mike Davenport had a way about him and the kids respected him. He was a good friend, and she could count on him to be reasonable.

She wove her way down the hall, keeping an eye out for Jason. She spied him in front of his locker with a fellow student she knew to be a close friend. As soon as he caught sight of her, he grabbed Mason's arm and hustled him off in the opposite direction. She'd expected no less. Why make things easy. At least he was at school and not lying bludgeoned and bleeding in an alley somewhere.

The start of school bell pealed and more students and teachers flooded the hallway. The same hallway she had traversed as a teenager. When the town had been gang free, but not without it's bad boys. Guys like Chase. She'd leaned against these very lockers, in this same hallway, willing Chase Porter to notice her. She hadn't been subtle. Cringing at the memories, she pressed a steadying hand against her stomach and waited while students filed past her. Live and learn. People weren't allowed do-overs. She could only go forward. Stand her ground. Continue to make a difference.

She stepped into her classroom and pushed the memories away. They had no place here. Learning happened here. Discussions, debates, and theories were welcomed and encouraged here. Every voice heard.

Chase Porter wasn't the only one considered good at his job.

****

All day, Lily tried, as unobtrusively as possible, to monitor how Jason was coping without alerting the other students. Jason did his teenage part—he avoided her like the plague.

After the last student filed through the door at the end of the day, Lily flopped back in her chair, closed her eyes, and willed her tense muscles to relax. She scooped the mass of tangled curls off her sweaty neck hoping for a little relief from the unseasonably warm heat.

During lunch, she'd managed to track down Mike. As the School Liaison Officer, he knew the students, developed relationships with them. At last, a cooperative ear. Together, they'd cooked up a plan involving her continued monitoring. She'd keep track of any noteworthy occurrences and coordinate with the police as they continued with their investigation. She could live with that.

Ten minutes after gathering up her stuff and trying not to envision gang bangers around every corner, Lily navigated her way into a parking spot on Main Street, close to Kate's Closet. The trendy, tiny, but always busy boutique was run by Kate Logan, proprietor, sympathetic ear, irreverent man-basher, and best friend.

Just inside the door, Lily paused to finger the folds of a beautiful cashmere coat perfect for the cooler autumn temperatures sure to hit any day, the cost of which would have her eating peanut butter and jelly for a month. With a sigh, she let go of the coat.

"Deciding against a little retail therapy are we?" Kate whispered from behind her.

Lily closed her eyes and let the comforting scent of wild spices waft around her before turning around. "Got it in one."

"New neighbors will do that to a gal."

"Ah, so I guess you've heard, huh?"

Kate gave her shoulder a small squeeze. "Have you run into him yet?"

Lily reached out a hand to stroke the fabric of a shirt laid out on a display table. "Oh, yeah. Twice."

Kate groaned, then started to steer her toward the door. "This sounds like a story best told over a horrifically sinful dessert."

"Oh God, I must look pathetic if you're offering to eat something fattening."

"I have been known to indulge for a good cause."

"Then we should indulge away."

"Come on, let's see what Mary has to offer today."

"I should protest, for your sake. I know you're busy." Her hands clenched around the strap of her purse. "But I need a friend and cake, or pie, or a baker's dozen of something sugary."

Lily waited while Kate spoke to her assistant.

She didn't want to go home, didn't want to face the possibility of running into Chase. She didn't want him next door, on her street, or in her town. She didn't want to remember. To remember what it had been like to be with him. And she most definitely didn't want to remember what it had been like to be without him.

Kate came up and gave Lily a tight hug. "Come on, let's go." She waved at a customer making her way to the till. "You know, I've got to admit—I'm dying of curiosity."

"Trust me when I say, your curiosity can't possibly do him justice."

"Really? No bald spot, beer belly, or horribly disfiguring scars?"

"Not hardly. He has muscles they haven't given a name to yet."

"The nerve."

"I know!"

"And how is it you've come to be an authority on his muscles?"

"I baked him muffins."

Kate stopped just outside the door of Kate's Closet. "Pardon me?"

Lily kept walking.

Kate caught up. "You baked the man muffins? Chase Porter, the one who used to live here, Chase Porter? The one who ditched you, Chase Porter? The one who stole your dream house out from under you, Chase Porter?"

Lily winced. "I fully appreciate the magnitude of that stupidity, believe me. I was being neighborly." She fought the rush of color crawling up her neck. She very carefully checked for oncoming traffic and avoided eye contact while she picked her way across the busy street.

"Neighborly?"

She paused at the door of Mary's before risking

a glance at Kate.

Kate didn't believe in wasting time or breath. "Because, in my mind, this type of delicate undertaking, which involves the asking of a certain individual to go the hell back to where he came from, is not accompanied by home baked goods."

Lily pushed open the door to Mary's and, for once, remained oblivious to the sumptuous smells of home baked cinnamon buns, Saskatoon berry pie, and freshly brewed coffee. She shot Kate a keep-it-down look before heading for the relative privacy of a back booth. She scowled at the vase with the one dusty, plastic red rose. Didn't that just kick it? So apropos. She reached for the one-page, laminated menu every regular knew by heart.

Kate snatched it out of her hand and laid it down.

"I know." Lily forced a fake smile as she finger waved to the mother of a student seated on the other side of the cafe. Out of the corner of her mouth, she said, "I was trying to be casual. Give the impression I couldn't care less he'd returned out of the blue."

Kate winked at Mr. Halliday as he hobbled by with his cane on his way to his regular table. She turned back to Lily. "And you figured baked goods would accomplish that? You couldn't have phoned for advice?"

"Can we move on from the muffins already?"

"Okay! Done obsessing about the muffins." Kate lifted her hands up in mock surrender. "For now."

"What's this, you gals looking for some home cooking?"

Kate smiled up at their server. "Hi Mary. I think for today only, we're looking for something a little more sinful and decadent."

"Well, you've come to the right place. I'll have you fixed up in no time with something guaranteed to put some flesh on those skinny bones of yours."

Kate shuddered. "Mary, please keep in mind there are only two of us."

"Oh you! You never gain an ounce." With a swat and an evil grin she ambled away.

"Why does no one ever take me seriously?"

"Gee, I wonder."

"So, what happened with Chase? Come on, spill."

"There's not much to tell." Lily traced a fingertip over a jagged scar carved into the Formica tabletop. "Things…came up, and I needed to discuss some theories with him."

Kate's eyebrows lifted. "Theories?"

Lily picked at an imaginary speck on the saltshaker. "Yes, theories." She reached for her cup and took a cautious sip of Mary's excellent coffee.

Kate crossed her arms and frowned. "What have you done?"

"Nothing. I needed to make it clear I couldn't care less that he's waltzed back into town. But things kind of went downhill once he opened the door all dripping wet and gorgeous. And time stopped and I felt sixteen years old again. But then he opened his mouth and started issuing orders. Believe me, I understand the severity of the situation. But when he touched me? I don't know…there was something." She flopped back against the booth and sighed.

Kate sat unblinking. "The man's been back in town for twenty-four hours. Why do you need theories? The severity of what situation?"

"Oh believe me, I'll get to that horrible part in a second."

Kate didn't move. "And there was touching?"

"Well, not really touching. He tucked a strand of hair behind my ear. That was all. I shouldn't have mentioned it. It was nothing." She lifted her shoulders in what she hoped passed for a nonchalant shrug and picked up her coffee cup. Set it down. "Okay, I threatened to shove an umbrella up his butt and I left. No big deal."

Kate nodded in perfect understanding. "No big deal. Because you're always threatening people with umbrellas."

"He started it by calling me a Mary Poppins do-gooder." She rubbed her forehead and let out a deep sigh. "I'm as pathetic today as I was back then."

"Lily, you were a teenager." Kate reached over to pat her hand. "Of course you were pathetic."

"And now?"

"Well, you did bake him muffins and threaten bodily harm with an umbrella."

Lily rolled her eyes. "I know. Like I said, pathetic."

"Honey, more like nuts, with a side order of crazy."

"You don't know the half of it."

Kate leaned in further. "Tell me everything. Leave no detail untold. And don't think for one second I've forgotten about the 'dripping wet' bit."

****

Chase abandoned the box marked "kitchen" in favor of the one labeled "files", choosing work over unpacking plates and spoons. Box opened, he pulled out the first file and settled in at the rickety kitchen table. After skimming through his personal notes, he tossed the file onto the table, plucked the next one out of the box. He rifled through the pages until he came across a picture. RT's tattooed face, with its permanent lip curl, mocked him. He separated it from the rest of the papers and positioned it on the table in front of him.

Okay, best case scenario, tomorrow Raphael Tessier would walk through the doors of the Aspen Lake Police Department and turn himself in. Yeah, while he was at it, he'd wish for a winning lotto ticket, the Leafs to win the Cup, and a fish "this" big.

Worst case scenario, RT would slither back underground, leaving Chase tracking a shadow or searching in circles for months. All the while, he'd be stuck living next door to Lily, which ranked Number Two on his worst-shit-possible scale right under getting shot.

He rose to his feet and swatted at one of the huge cobwebs dangling from the grimy ceiling. The mess stuck to his heat damp fingers and refused to shake loose. How friggin' apt was that? Had he really thought he could drive back into town and not get tangled up with Lily? The same Lily, by the way, he'd had sex with exactly once. In high school. Ten years ago. On his way out of town.

He eyed the stack of boxes in his living room. The sweltering evening hours stretched out before him one pitiful cardboard box at a time. Hot, sweaty, and frustrated, he tugged up the bottom of his frayed gray T-shirt, swiped at the moisture collecting across his forehead. What the hell had he been thinking agreeing to come back here? Man, he needed a beer. Or many beers. And a CAT scan. Or a shrink. Again.

And damn his scheming excuse of a realtor to hell. A quaint, post-Victorian home, his ass. Unless crumbling and broken-down constituted quaint. In that case, he'd nailed the description. Fine by him, he didn't have forever in mind. A couple years tops, unless he hit the transfer to anywhere else lottery. He hated tranquil and quiet. He preferred noise and movement. Life after nine in the evening. Anonymity.

And more than one degree of separation between him and his high school sweetheart, for fuck sake.

The muscles in his thigh contracted, but this time he refused to acknowledge the ache. To make matters worse, someone knocked on his front door. Just what he needed, a repeat of this morning's debacle with Lily. He mopped at the back of his damp neck and considered not answering. The person on the other side of the door knocked again. He listened as the doorknob turned, the door swung open, and someone entered uninvited. Chase swore under his breath and prepared to head off his intruder. He wasn't in the mood for company. He got about four feet before his uninvited guest rounded the corner.

Chase should have known he'd show up sooner rather than later.

"So the rumors are true?"

Chase let out a burst of laughter. "Depends on the rumor." In his experience, Aspen Lake didn't suffer from a shortage of rumors.

The older man shrugged. "I knocked. No one answered, so I let myself in."

Chase eyed the man in front of him, registered the thinning gray hair, lined face, and the paunch. "I can see that."

"So, you're back."

"Yep." Chase approached, held out his hand and a warm, firm grip greeted his. "It's good to see you, Stan."

"Chase. It's been too long." Chase grinned as his mentor gave his hand an extra squeeze. Sergeant Knight released his hand and looked over Chase's newly acquired space. "It needs some work, all right. You buy it?"

Chase snorted. "Not on your life. Renting."

"Ah."

Yes, ah. Only Stan Knight could crowd a boatload of meaning into a two-letter word.

Chase shrugged. "Come on, let me buy you a drink." He led Stan through to the kitchen and headed straight to the fridge. He pulled out a diet soda, passing it to Stan. He grabbed a beer for himself. "How's retired life?"

"Not worth mentioning." Stan grimaced before indulging in a long drink of soda. "Thanks."

"And Ruth?"

"Fine." The older man pulled out a kitchen chair, sat down, and picked up the picture of Raphael Tessier, let it drop. "Are we about done with the small talk now?"

Chase smirked. "I don't know. You must have some fish stories? How's the golf game coming?"

"Don't fish. Don't golf. Don't have plans to start either one." He crossed his arms over his belly and settled back. "Hear you ran into some trouble over at the school yesterday."

"You could say that."

Stan nodded at the picture of Tessier. "That him?"

"Yeah."

"Ugly bastard."

Chase quirked an eyebrow in agreement. "His tactics are uglier."

"And Lily? She okay?"

"She's fine." Better than fine, in fact.

"And the kid?"

"As far as I know, yeah. Mike Davenport is handling that end of things." Chase pulled out a chair. "You know him?"

"Not personally, no. Had dealings with his father though, when I was on the job." He straightened in his chair and maneuvered it closer to the table. "And the older boy. Trouble every which way from Sunday, that one."

Chase chugged down a swallow of beer before replying. "I hear his home life's not the best."

Stan tipped his head, and Chase got that bug under glass feeling. "You'd probably find you had a lot in common."

"So everyone keeps saying." But he wasn't looking to trade war stories with a thirteen-year-old. He didn't want to acknowledge a connection of any kind. He didn't want to feel anything.

"Can't help the truth."

But you could ignore it. He focused on the stained wallpaper over Stan's left shoulder and changed the subject. "He's mixed up in something nasty, for sure."

"How bad?" Stan leaned in. "Mind?" He picked up a couple of sheets of paper and scanned them.

"Be my guest." Chase shifted closer to the table. "Bad with a capital B."

Chase gave the old man a little background and went over a few facts. Stan was good at connecting the dots. Always had been. He'd been a damn fine cop and made a very frustrated retiree. Chase planned to take advantage of the fact. He needed Stan's expertise and his help.

Stan remained silent, listening. He was good at that, too. He regurgitated the facts until he had it all straight. "That father of his isn't going to be any help."

"That's where you come in. I was hoping you'd be able to help keep a discreet eye on Jason."

"Discreet, huh?"

"Yeah. Very discreet. As in, I never asked you."

"About time." He grinned. "It'd be my pleasure."

Chase didn't grin back. "These are the worst of the worst, Stan. You need to be careful not to spook Jason or the Brotherhood."

"You're worried over the boy's motives?"

"I don't know how he fits in yet. Could be he's looking to be a part of a gang. But I'm not convinced one way or another."

Stan shook his head. "Such a waste. And you know how I feel about wasted potential."

"Yeah, it pisses you off. I remember."

"Hey, worked on you."

"Yes, it did. I'll always be grateful for it."

"Well, never mind about that. Someone had to keep you fed and watered, not to mention on the straight and narrow. Ruth's anxious to see you, by the way."

"I'll be by soon."

Stan pointed a finger in his direction. "Bring flowers. She likes flowers. There are never enough flowers."

"Will do."

"And I'll keep my eye on the boy." Stan stood up and Chase followed his lead.

"Thanks, I appreciate it."

"You watch your back."

"Count on it." Chase appreciated the weight of Stan's warm hand on his shoulder.

He promised a visit and waved his mentor and friend off, then snagged another beer out of his fridge. He escaped out his backdoor, and collapsed on the top step of his crumbling back stoop with its view of the *Untamed Wilderness*. The waist high weeds mocked him. Unpacked boxes demanded his attention. His furniture arrived tomorrow. He had a kid to worry about, a sexy neighbor to avoid, and a gang member to track down. He downed a long, cold guzzle of beer.

The job. His job. Doing it well. That was all that mattered. Period. End of story. He'd do whatever it took to bring Tessier down.

His attention strayed to the tall, leafy hedge separating him from his sexy, off limits next-door neighbor. Wanting didn't mean having, and his dick could damn well get used to the idea.

He shifted, stretched out his legs and gave himself some room. A bullet in the thigh was nothing compared to the threat of having to rip his heart out a second time. He rubbed a hand over his chest. But knowing it and using the fact to stem old memories was a magic trick he'd failed to learn. Knowing it didn't douse the heat or curb his longings. It only made him hotter.

Chapter Four

Chase perched on the edge of his chair while he shuffled papers and signed his name in the appropriate spots. A thrum of excitement erased any lasting remnants of his bad attitude from the night before. He let the feeling build with each pen stroke. His instincts told him Raphael Tessier was still close by. He'd climbed out of his hole for a reason, and RT wasn't one to leave until he got what he wanted.

Chase knew him. He'd put everything he had into shutting Raphael Tessier and the Prairie Brotherhood down. His professional knowledge and experience coupled with his drive made him a formidable opponent, but he'd had limited success flushing him out.

Cue yesterday.

His transfer to the backwaters had put his search on hold. Or, so he'd thought. He never dreamed Tessier would drop into his lap.

"Glad to have you on board, Chase. In light of recent events, we can really use your expertise and experience."

Chase nodded and passed the stack of papers to Staff Sergeant Jeff Weins. "I'm looking forward to working with everyone here. We'll get it under control."

"Yesterday's events are only a sample of what's been boiling up around here." Jeff shook his head as he absently straightened papers. "We need to shut it down before it explodes in our faces."

Chase pushed his chair back when Jeff stood. "See you Monday."

Jeff offered his hand. "Monday it is. Mike will give you a bit more of a tour than you got the other day and introduce you to any of the staff you haven't already met. It's a good group." The staff sergeant reached into his pocket and pulled out a ringing phone. "Sorry, but I've got to take this." He lifted a hand in farewell as he made his way out the door. "Gord. Thanks for calling me back..."

Mike Davenport eased past Jeff. "Chase. Welcome aboard." The big blond man held out his hand and grinned.

"Thanks."

"Do you have a minute to go over a couple of things?"

At Chase's nod, Mike set a couple of files down on the table and pulled up a chair. "Here's what we have on recent gang activity in the area. We're noticing an increased presence, for sure. Yesterday is a bit of a puzzle, though. Not what we're used to seeing."

Chase flipped through the file, skimmed over the details, took note of some dates. He tossed the file back on the table. "The Prairie Brotherhood gets off on intimidation, the bloody, terrorizing kind. If you're asking me, they're just getting started. You've got a noticeable increase in graffiti, a surge in vandalism and auto thefts. Those are key markers in establishing a gang presence. It means they're recruiting and then initiating the newest wannabes. The summer is winding down and so is the tourist season, so we'll see what happens next." He straightened up the file and ran his finger along the edge as he studied the man sitting across from him. "What can you tell me about Jason McCarran?"

"Jason? Sad story there and exactly the type of

kid these assholes would look at."

And the type of kid Lily would pick to champion, one written off by everyone else. Wasn't Chase a case in point, cast off by everyone else until she'd shone her light on him? Chase shifted in his chair. She'd looked past all his baggage, treated him like he was someone with something to offer. He'd repaid her faith in him by disappearing without a word.

"Has he been in trouble before?"

"He's actually a straight up kid. A lot of attitude, but he's managed to stay on track. No, the problem is his home life sucks, mother's passed away—cancer—alcoholic father who doesn't give a shit, and an older brother who's been in and out of jail. He's at that age where it could go either way if the wrong influences take hold, know what I mean?"

Yeah, he knew. Hadn't he lived it? Chase rubbed his hands down his thighs before putting them to rest on the table. "This doesn't sound like recruiting to me. Doesn't fit the pattern." He shook his head. "This is more intimidation. This kid has something, or knows something, and we need to find out what's going on fast because the one thing I do know is they aren't going to stop until they get it."

Anyone standing in the Brotherhood's way risked serious harm, including pretty strawberry blonde teachers with invincibility issues. His guts cramped up at the host of possible outcomes, each one more brutal and bloody than the last. The Prairie Brotherhood did not issue idle threats. What they considered their laws and mandates dictated instant and vicious action. Anyone at odds paid, or a member of his or her family paid, someone always paid and paid in blood.

"Whatever it is, Jason isn't talking. Not to me, not to Lily, not to anyone."

"Well, he'd better talk to someone or he's going to come up against the likes of which nightmares are made. Alone, this kid doesn't stand a chance."

"Lily and I will work on him. See if we can get him to open up. We've got plans to meet. We'll figure something out."

Meet?

Chase scratched the side of his neck. Did he want to know? Not really. It was none of his business. Except, the hell it wasn't. What if Davenport's judgment was compromised or impaired? Couldn't he see the best place for Lily was as far away from Jason as possible? "You're sure that's wise? Encouraging her involvement?"

Davenport laughed. "Try stopping her. Lily's...she's passionate about her kids." He dipped his head. "And she's a soft touch until you cross her, then, look out."

"You don't say." Passionate. He scrubbed a hand over his jaw. About her kids. The list had better be that short. The thought brought him up short. He'd been back for what? Thirty-six hours? And already he was losing his mind, along with his perspective.

"Don't worry about Lily. I'll keep an eye on her. Make sure she stays out of trouble."

Don't worry about Lily? That was like asking a member of the counter terrorism unit to chill, or the defense to quit tackling the guy with the ball. Not gonna happen. Hadn't he given it his best shot for ten years? Look where it'd gotten him. Right back where he'd started. And if it came down to worrying or panting after her, he was going with worrying. For all their sakes.

"No offense, but we all need to worry. It's not every day the power behind the Death List comes to town."

"The Death List?" Mike straightened as his grin faded, replaced by a hardness Chase recognized and acknowledged with an explanation.

"Tessier's list. No one sees it but him and two

others. He decides who and when. As for how, there's only one way off the list. On your knees, hands bound behind your back waiting for a bullet to be fired into your brain at close range."

"Your partner? Conrad Hutton." The name was said with respect, in honor of a fallen fellow officer, and he appreciated it. Conrad had been a damn good cop, one who hadn't deserved to die the way he had. No one did.

"Yeah." Add to that, Conrad Hutton had been a last minute substitution for Chase. He should have died in that alley not his partner.

That's why two years, two months and six days ago, he'd created his own list.

****

Lily tapped out a stress pattern on her steering wheel. It was Friday. The weekend loomed, a widening black abyss of what the heck was she supposed to do now. On one hand, she worried about Jason being on his own for a solid forty-eight hours, the sky being the limit on the amount of trouble lurking around corners for him. On the other hand, she had her new and know-it-all neighbor to avoid. She lifted the hair off the back of her heated neck and exhaled, loud and long. She couldn't shake the sense of unease camped out in her stomach.

The empty school parking lot stretched out before her as she mulled over what to do. She hummed and hawed for a good few seconds before deciding one quick dash by Jason's house to check on things wasn't going to bring about the end of the world. Plus, it classified as being on her route home, in a roundabout kind of way, if she stretched things.

Her very bad feeling ballooned into foreboding. A quick pass by his house would reassure her. Mute her new nightmarish imagination. The likelihood of catching sight of him was miniscule. But before she opened the very nice bottle of Chardonnay chilling in her fridge, a little covert drive-by couldn't hurt. While she was at it, she might as well take a run past his best friend's house. Reassured, she'd head home, take a cool shower, and relax with a glass of wine.

Jason would never know she was checking up on him. His attitude made it abundantly clear he didn't appreciate her nosing into his business. Other than typical classroom interaction, he avoided her along with everyone else in a position of authority, right down to the janitor. She hoped Mike met with more success. Not that she was close to giving up.

She steered her car in the direction of Jason's house, cranking up the Doc Walker song playing on the radio. To the strains of *Beautiful Life,* she turned the corner onto the street one over from Jason's. Her very bad feeling morphed into dread.

The same rusted out sedan from yesterday blocked off part of the road. She eased up on the gas and coasted past slow enough to see Jason corralled in the middle of the evil little pack. She slammed on the brakes, then jerked the car over to the side of the road, right in front of where they all stood.

Lily grabbed her cell phone off the seat beside her. Her fingers shook as she missed buttons, pressed wrong ones. Someone kicked at her passenger side door, sending her little Bug and her heart into convulsions. Finally, she came up with the right nine-one-one combination. She shouted a location into her phone a second before the glass of the passenger side window shattered.

She screamed and covered her head with her hands. Through her fingers, she heard the lock release. The passenger door open. Someone reached across the seat to rip her phone out of her hand.

The need to escape consumed her. She clawed at her door handle until it burst open. Tumbling out, she gained her feet, and scrambled around to face the small group of men.

"You're too late. I called the police. Told them where we are." She sucked in air as she inched her way around to the front of her car. She slammed her hands on the cherry red hood. "Now, back away from him before I start screaming bloody murder."

Jason stared at her with equal parts relief and dread. She tried to reassure him with a quick glance before she put out a bracing hand in the direction of his attackers. She recognized them, all of them, as the same men from yesterday. Raphael Tessier stepped forward and she started to shake.

"Go ahead and scream, lady. Make it interesting." A glint of metal drew her attention to his hand. Panic ate her good intentions. The deadly switchblade rested in his long, lean fingers. His hand was steady, not so much as a quiver. He twirled it. "Do you have any idea how much damage I can do with a knife?"

"Stop it. Don't come any closer." Lily flinched as he advanced. In the distance, someone yelled a warning. A neighbor? She didn't dare take her eyes off his tattooed face.

"You're beginning to piss me off, lady. Bad, bad move." He gestured, and the other three men shifted into position behind him, herding Jason into the middle. Raphael Tessier lifted a hand, and the man closest to Jason made a grab for him. Jason tried to ram an elbow into his attacker's stomach.

"He's going to give me what I want. One way or another." Tessier jerked his head in Jason's direction. "Get him in the car." He pointed a finger at her. "Leave. Unless you want to join us."

"Leave him alone." Her words burst in the air, horror-stricken, and with enough volume to get noticed. She watched Jason stagger, taking his attacker with him. The contents of her stomach curdled.

"No? Gonna stop me, little teacher?" His top lip curled. His dark eyes raked over her body.

"You don't scare me." *He terrified her to death.*

"I scare you plenty." He closed in, broader and taller than a few seconds ago. The knife blade glittered in the sunshine, sparkled. She froze.

He kept coming. "I don't even have to lay a hand on you to do it." He never took his eyes off hers. "Cut his finger off."

The casual order speared into her brain.

"No! Don't hurt him. Please!" She lunged for Jason and slammed up against Raphael Tessier's chest. He spun her in a clumsy pirouette. Her back smashed up against his front, with his knife arm encircling her throat.

She sank her teeth into his arm.

A hiss of breath exploded from him. His "Bitch" caught the air, sailed away. His knife clattered to the ground. She didn't waste time.

"Jason! Run!" She started screaming and didn't stop. She slammed the heel of her wedged sandal against Tessier's instep and rammed an elbow into his hard stomach. She wrenched around, brought her knee up, attempted to slam it into his groin. He dodged, and she missed her mark, but he backed up a step. She heard others in the background, on the periphery, threatening. She shoved as hard as she could and sent him back another step. The gap gave her enough room to slip around him. Strong fingers curled around her arm. He dragged her back. His wicked backhand caught her by surprise. Pain exploded behind her eyes. She tried to blink past it and failed as the ground came up to meet her.

"Get him in the fucking car already." Her scalp screamed in protest as his fist twisted into her hair and yanked. "Stay out of my business." Her head knocked against the sidewalk. Dazed, she struggled to focus on his retreating boots.

"Jason!" Slapping her hands against the concrete, she pushed to her knees. Jason, arms flailing, legs kicking, fought to stay out of the car. Two neighbors charged into the fray and got shoved back. More yelling. The flash of a blade.

"He's got a knife." The screams tore from her throat as she wobbled to her feet and lost sight of Jason. If they got him into their vehicle, she'd never get him out. Sirens sounded in the distance. A wave of dizziness blinded her. She stumbled. Back on her feet, she focused on Tessier as he and his men scrambled to get into their car. Terror gripped her when the doors slammed shut. The smell of burnt rubber assaulted her nose as their car sped away. More screeching tires. Doors slamming. More screaming. Her throat on fire.

"Jason! He's in the car!" She stumbled out into the street.

"Lily." Solid arms wrapped around her waist. "Lily, listen to me." She struggled and the pressure increased. "Lily, calm down."

"Jason!" She pounded on her restraints. Tried to catch her breath.

She grabbed at the iron bands holding her in place, tried to peel them off, to follow the car. They held her tight. She couldn't move, couldn't catch her breath in a mudslide of panic. Had to break free. Had to save Jason. "He's in the car."

"Lily, listen to me." A voice close to her ear. Whispering. Demanding.

"Let me go." She tried to yank free.

"Lily, it's me, Chase. Everything is under control." More whispering. Soothing this time.

Couldn't they hear her? She needed to go after Jason. She had to—

"Jason isn't in the car. He's safe."

Chase's voice. Chase was here. He was a cop. He could help her. She twisted in his arms and grabbed handfuls of his shirt.

"No, I saw—"

Chase pulled her close. The press of warmth allowed a hint of sanity to return. Strong hands kneaded her arms, travelled over her back.

"Jason is not in the car. Do you hear me?" His hands moved to cup her face. Blue eyes stared into hers and continued to hold her gaze until her focus centered on him, on his face.

"Breathe. In. Out. Nice and slow."

She tried, but it was harder than it should have been to pull air into her lungs. She kept seeing Jason surrounded, helpless, being dragged to their car.

"The kid took off at top speed in the opposite direction. We're searching for him, he can't have gone far. He's safe enough for now." A police officer approached, asked a question, got an answer, and retreated.

"For now," she whispered. She shut her eyes and concentrated on breathing. She pried them open to stare into Chase's. "But what about a half an hour from now, what about two hours from now, or tomorrow?"

"Lily, I know it's asking a lot, but you have to calm down and trust me. We're not going to let anything happen to this kid." His hand gripped her chin, keeping it in place, as he studied her cheek. She ignored his mumbled curses and tugged his hand away.

"His name is Jason." She doused the urge to scream it at the top of her lungs. His. Name. Is. Jason.

"Jason. We're not going to let anything happen to Jason. I promise."

"Then where were you five minutes ago? When they tried to kidnap him? Or worse." Her voice hiccupped over the words. "Where were you then?"

The tears slipped down, and she was powerless to stop them. "He needs help. He needs you. He needs someone to go after him. To look after him. And he hasn't got anybody."

****

Chase clung to his control by his fingernails. Her tears destroyed him. The mark blossoming on her cheek drove him to the edge of stupid. He couldn't afford stupid. Stupid got people killed. He stepped back, put a hand on her arm, and guided her to his truck. A second patrol car rounded the corner.

He tried to dampen down the cocktail of adrenaline and fury coursing through his system and failed. Someone would pay, and pay dearly, for the marks on her, for causing the terror giving her the shakes. There was no hole deep enough, no forest vast enough, no mountain huge enough to hide Raphael Tessier now.

His out of control feelings scared the shit out of him. He focused on the now, on the crime, on the officer approaching once again and expecting coherent answers. He offered a brief explanation to his question, watched him walk away.

"Are you going to be okay?"

"I'm fine. It's Jason I'm worried about." She swiped the spent tears off her cheeks and blinked back the newcomers.

"Okay, then. They went in opposite directions. He's safe for now." He sighed. "The police are here. Don't worry, we'll find him."

He lifted her up onto the seat of his truck and searched her eyes for further signs of shock. Her breathing was better, the shaking was subsiding, but he reached behind the front seat for an old jacket he kept there and wrapped it around her.

He strove for unemotional and objective, but found it impossible. He tugged the coat closer around her shoulders.

He pointed to her cheek. "And this doesn't look fine to me." The bruise on her soft skin cut him to the quick.

She flinched. "It is. I am. But I want to know Jason is safe." Once again, tears filled her eyes. "What if he's hurt? They had a knife. What if they find him?"

Knives. Beatings. Terrorism. It made him sick to his stomach. Chase stepped closer, his thumbs wiping away the overflowing tears. "I promise our number one priority will be to find Jason and keep him safe. We'll also go after the guys who did this to him. I promise. Jason will be okay." He spoke succinctly and calmly. "We will do everything possible to protect him." Or die trying. It's what cops did. But she didn't need to hear that.

"You promise?" She sniffed.

"Yes." Against his better judgment, he was ready to promise her anything.

"All right."

Chase knew she spared no thought for herself, for her own safety, her concern solely for her student. But he was concerned. She'd chosen, she'd taken a stand, and it was going to cost her. She had no idea what happened to those who got in the way of something the Prairie Brotherhood wanted.

He shifted, and his hip brushed against her thigh. She was upset. She didn't notice. He did. His blood began to sing a different tune, and his fingers stopped the gentle massage of her palms. His muscles tightened, his jaw locked, he started a slow count backward from one hundred, willing his hands to let go.

Lily glanced in the direction of the police vehicle parking along the side of the road. He moved back as Lily jumped down from the seat of his truck, his jacket slipping from her shoulders. Watched her rush toward Mike Davenport.

"Lily, are you all right?" asked Mike. He grabbed hold of her arms and pulled her into a big hug.

Chase's toxic mix of adrenaline and desire coagulated into something a lot less friendly.

"I'm fine. Mike, they came after Jason again. The same men who attacked him before. You have to find him."

"Slow down. How about you start at the beginning." Mike acknowledged Chase's presence from across the pavement. "Chase."

"Mike." His fingers wrapped into fists. He just barely resisted the urge to cross the road and rip the man's hands off Lily.

He stood guard while Lily explained what had happened. He held back while Mike soothed Lily until her recollection of the events became coherent and ordered. He ground his molars to powder while Mike comforted her, pulled her close, and wrapped his arms around her. Again. But that was nothing compared to the bolt of repressed possessiveness that surged through him when she hugged him back.

He knew the way Mike watched him over the top of Lily's head he was giving too much away. Knew from the way Mike kept his eyes on him as he gave her another quick hug before letting her go.

"Lily, here's what we're going to do. As soon as I finish up here, I help look for Jason. We'll also be looking for the suspects. I'll need you to come in and make a statement, but tomorrow should be good. Write things down when you get home, and if you remember anything else, call me." Chase felt the constable's eyes land on him like a physical punch. "You've got my number, so use it if you need to. And don't worry, we'll make sure Jason is safe. Can you hang on a minute while I talk to Chase?"

Chase stayed planted to the cement while Mike crossed over to him. He kept his eyes on Lily as she turned to another police officer, to give descriptions of the gang members who had attacked her. Attacked her and a thirteen-year-old child. If he hadn't happened on the scene, the situation would have escalated—kidnapping, bloodshed, or worse. His stomach heaved.

"How much did you see?" asked Mike.

"Enough to know the boy's in real trouble with some very nasty people."

"The Prairie Brotherhood?"

"Yes, same as yesterday. I recognized the markers, the tats, the clothes. Raphael Tessier, of course. Yeah, it's the Brotherhood."

"Shit."

"That doesn't even begin to cover it."

"And Lily?"

"She's interfered twice, and if they think the kid's confided in her, they'll act on it."

"They'll come after her, too."

"No doubt about it."

"Well, fuck."

"We've got to find a way to protect them both."

"You coming into the station?"

"After I get Lily home."

Mike raised his eyebrows. "And how does Lily feel about that?"

None of your fucking business, buddy. Instead of voicing his thought, he made a stab at diplomacy. "I'm here, and you guys need to get busy tracking Jason and the bad guys. I'll make sure she gets home safe." He flashed a lot of teeth, but it didn't come close to being friendly.

Mike looked to the side, nodded. "You do anything to mess her up further, I won't be a happy camper."

A muscle jerked along Chase's jaw line. "And what is it you think I'm going to do?"

Mike moved a step closer. "I'm saying you're looking a bit fierce there, pal. You might want to dial it down a notch."

"And maybe you don't have enough experience with this shit to know what you're dealing with...pal."

Mike's eyes narrowed. "You don't know me, so don't make assumptions you got no basis for."

Once again, Chase wondered about the relationship between Mike and Lily. Wondered if it passed the bonds of friendship. Because, if it did, things were going to get real complicated, real fast.

Chase leaned in closer. "These guys do whatever they have to do, including killing people, to get what they want."

"And maybe we don't need Lily knowing that right at this time." Mike stared straight at him. "So like I said, bring it down a notch."

He didn't like it when the other person was right, and he was the idiot. He glared down the tree-lined street and noticed people, concerned townspeople, gathered here and there. He glanced at Lily, pale but still standing, talking to a uniformed officer. She smiled and accepted a steaming cup from a bystander. He was being an asshole. He had no right to be protective of Lily above what his job demanded. Lily had drawn that line in the dirt very clearly this morning.

"I'll get her home, make sure she's safe, and I'll be in touch."

"Good." Mike walked away, leaving Chase to follow behind.

"Lily, I think I've got all the information I need, so you're free to head on home."

"You'll let me know when you find him?"

Mike put a hand on her shoulder. "You bet." He nodded briefly at Chase. "See you later."

Lily frowned. "Everything all right?"

Chase attempted to arrange his features into something resembling reassurance, shrugged and lied. “Everything’s good. Come on, I’ll take you home.”

“That’s okay, I’m fine.” Lily gestured toward her car. “I’ll drive.”

“Then I’ll follow you home.”

“That’s not necessary.”

“Yeah, it is.” In fact, the idea of seeing Lily home was fast tracking its way to essential.

“Chase, there’s no need. I said I was fine and I meant it. I’m fully capable of driving myself home.” Dismissing him she moved in the direction of her car.

“I know. But give your neighbors a break, let them see someone helping you home. They’re worried. It would go a long way toward reassuring everyone.”

Her eyes closed, and her shoulders dipped a degree. “Fine. Do whatever. I’m going home.”

Chase waited until she shut the door of her ridiculous little car before climbing into his truck. He slammed a hand against the wheel. He pulled out his phone and dialed Stan’s number. He had to find Raphael Tessier before Tessier did something to nudge him across the wrong side of that thin blue line. From doing something from which there was no crossing back.

Chapter Five

Lily sagged in relief as Chase's black truck sped past her house. The very last thing she needed was a scene with him. She plucked a shard of glass from the glittering pile covering the passenger seat, turned it over, and studied it before heaving it at the windshield.

Jason was in huge trouble, with nightmare etched all over it. She pulled the keys out of the ignition, but instead of opening the door, she slumped in her seat and let her head drop back. All her energy sapped, too tired to budge, she allowed her eyes to drift shut.

Nothing about this situation made any sense. The extremes and excessive lengths these people went to scrambled her brainwaves. She had no point of reference. No experience with knife-wielding gang members.

Cut his finger off.

Not a threat, an order. What had Chase called him? The Enforcer. She pressed her hands against her roiling stomach and breathed through the nausea. Raphael Tessier hadn't said it to scare her, but to torture her. Or to test her reaction? To see how far she'd go to protect Jason?

A light knock on the window jolted her upright. Chase's muffled "Lily" accompanying the second tap put a little of the fight back in her.

She shoved her car door open. "Are you trying to

push me over the edge?"

"Sorry, I didn't mean to startle you." He held out a hand.

She ignored it. "Startle me? You Texas-Chainsawed me." She waited for him to move. He didn't. Too tired to argue, she slapped her palm against his. He tugged until she stood toe-to-toe with him. Way, way too close.

"I wanted to make sure you were all right."

"We have these things here in the boondocks, they're called telephones. Or this thing called email?" Mercy, anything but up close and personal.

"I'm familiar with the options."

"Ow." She flinched as he brushed a thumb over the bruise on her cheek.

"I'm going to hurt whoever did this to you." He wasn't kidding. The promise deepened his eye color to a dizzying blue. Or maybe the dizzying part was a side-effect of everything, and Chase.

"Chase." She puffed out a breath. "Just...don't.

"Don't what? Don't care that gang members attacked and terrorized you? Don't—"

"Don't act like you care more because it's me who's involved."

"I do care more." He caught her arm as she pushed past. "Wait."

Lily eyed the long tan fingers wrapped around her arm before she willed herself to lift her head and look him in the eye. "Let go."

In an instant, his hand fell away. "Lily, what do you want me to say? Do you want me to forget we have a history?" He stepped to the right, blocking her path without touching her. "Is that what you want? Because I can't do that. I'm standing here right now because that's the one thing I can't do."

"Oh, please." She managed to look him straight in the eye, hold his gaze, and lie through her teeth. "How touching." She snorted. "You left, remember?

Ten years ago you up and walked away without a word. Fine, your choice." She lightly touched the bruise on her cheek. "Yes, they hurt me, but this pain is nothing compared to what I felt when you left. But hey, I got over it. I got over you. The past is staying in the past. So, never mind standing there all concerned telling me what you can or can't do because it's none of my business, not anymore."

She engineered her escape and, in the process, brushed up against his scent and his warmth, flashes of hot color against a frightening backdrop of fear. Strong, reassuring, and familiar, it beckoned her, called to her in a way she'd never forgotten. How embarrassing was that? She hurried her stride without glancing back.

In her rush, she almost stepped on the small black tangle of plastic lying outside her front door. She frowned and bent to get a closer look. When recognition hit, she clamped one hand over her mouth to stem the reaction. With the other, she reached out to pick up what was left of her mangled cell phone.

Footsteps sounded behind her, and she hesitated.

"Don't touch it." Chase put a restraining hand on her shoulder. She wanted to tip her head and rest her cheek against his hand. To lean on him. To let him deal with it.

Instead, she straightened up without touching her cell phone, the one Raphael Tessier had grabbed out of her hand. The one he'd given back.

She stifled a crazy, inappropriate desire to laugh, which didn't quite work. The realization Tessier had taken the time to drive by her house and leave her a message left her knees wobbling. They knew where she lived. A shiver flashed down her spine. Not that they couldn't have looked it up in the phone book, but still…

"Come here."

And she went because that's what shock did to a person, made them do things they'd sworn sixty seconds earlier weren't necessary or relevant. When he pulled her close and gathered her up in his arms, she clung to him like a tick on a dog.

"It's going to be okay. I promise." He smoothed a hand over her hair and down her back. Over and over again.

She pressed her face into his neck and mumbled, "As much as I want to believe you, I'm beginning to wonder." His hand clasped the back of her head and brought her closer. Brought his mouth next to her ear.

"Don't worry. I'm going to fix this." She let the words wash over her, calm her.

"Okay." It felt so good to be in his arms. So right. She willed her survival instincts to kick in. She backed up and put a psychological mile of space into two inches of physical distance. And he let her.

"Here, give me your keys." He held out a hand.

She didn't bother arguing, just handed them over.

He unlocked the door and stepped inside. He paused on the threshold, shoulder muscles tense. She knew because she was plastered to his back, recording every ripple. After a couple of seconds, he moved into her living room while she burrowed as close to him as she could get.

He gently pushed her aside. "I'll be right back. Stay put."

She heard him talking on his phone as he moved around her bungalow, meticulously checking every room, every nock and cranny, making sure nothing deadly lurked in the corners. Only then did he come back. She still stood in the same spot. He twined his fingers with hers and led her to her couch.

"Sit down before you fall down."

She sat. Not because she wanted to, but her legs agreed with him. His were fine and busy taking him somewhere else. From the rummaging sounds trickling out the back of the bungalow, she guessed he was in the kitchen. Next thing she knew, he set something down on the coffee table in front of her. She opened her eyes and spying the tumbler of juice, closed them again.

"Thanks," she said but didn't move. It required too much effort. All of a sudden, every muscle hurt, and her limbs felt like dead weights.

"Here, take these." He laid the painkillers in her palm, waited until she popped them into her mouth, then handed her the juice. "I'm going to put this bag of peas on your cheek, like a cold pack. It'll help with the swelling."

"Fine." The weight of the bag made her wince, but she agreed to hold it in place. She wanted to tell him to go, assure him she was fine, but she was so not fine. She couldn't force the words out. She needed him to stay. With all her heart, she needed the reassurance of his six-foot-one-inch policeman's body standing guard. And if the powers that be had any mercy at all, they wouldn't make her admit it out loud.

"Try and get some rest. I'm going to make a few calls." His hand brushed at some of her stray curls before he straightened from his perch on the coffee table.

She managed a faint nod and a silent prayer of thanks before she curled up on her comfy couch, exhausted but convinced actual sleep was beyond her.

****

Chase set the phone receiver back in its cradle. With clinical precision, he peeled his fingers off the handset one digit at a time and congratulated himself for resisting the urge to hurl it against the wall. He didn't understand it. What the hell did the Prairie Brotherhood want with this kid? Had he heard something, seen something? What could he possibly know that would send the Brotherhood scrambling? Bring Tessier out in the open?

He raked a hand through hair already standing on end. The Prairie Brotherhood was one of the most vicious organized adult gangs on the prairies. They didn't bother with petty shit. They were into drugs, hookers, grand theft auto, and murder. They were cold blooded, vicious and brutal in their dealings, but they weren't stupid. Whatever was happening, it was major. Somehow Jason, and now Lily, had ended up on their radar. And blips on the Prairie Brotherhood's radar screen tended to end up dead.

"Hey."

"Hey." He shut his eyes at the sound of her voice. He prayed he'd didn't look as wrecked as he felt. He did a quick mental health check before he faced her. Made sure he had all his ducks in a row before he asked, "How are you feeling?"

"A little less run over then I did an hour ago." She wrapped herself tighter into her fleece blanket. "Thanks."

He should have kept his eyes shut. Looking at her hurt worse than he could have imagined.

"No problem." *Liar.* The whole sleepy, tousled look she had going on caused him problems on every level. The exact reason he'd implemented a fuck and flee policy. He never, ever stuck around long enough to witness the vulnerable bits. Now, here she stood in her cozy little kitchen, strawberry blonde curls falling here and there, her eyes a bit drowsy, looking all soft and homey huddled in her fuzzy blue blanket. The perfect manifestation of his favorite nightmare.

The purplish blue bruise spreading across her cheek curled his fists into tight balls. Bruises and the promise of them were the reason he'd left her in the first place.

"Did Mike phone?" She stepped further into the room.

"No. Not yet." *Mike.* That name was fast becoming his least favorite word.

"I was hoping they'd have found him by now." She leaned her head back and rolled her shoulders.

He couldn't stand it, the thought of her getting hurt, which is why his common sense didn't kick in until halfway across the room and four steps too late to do him any good. He hated the idea of her injured, worried, facing the possibility of more devastating news. He laid a hand against her cheek, let it slip back down when he felt her stiffen, and was thankful for the reminder, for his cue to leave.

"We'll find him."

"I know."

Tempted to touch her again, he shoved his hands into his pockets. "Lily, I promise you. We'll find him. I know what I'm doing. I'm the best chance this kid has against the Prairie Brotherhood."

She huffed out a breath. "And why is that? Exactly."

He shook his head.

"Tell me. Why is that?"

"There's no point—"

"There is every point. I'm involved in this whether you want me to be or not. So maybe, if we share information, we can figure this out."

No. Way. In. Hell. "That's not going to happen."

He pushed down the anger that clawed at him and, God help him, the fear. The damage they were capable of...she had no idea. The problem was, he did. First-hand knowledge. And this was Lily, his Lily, being dragged into the middle of who knew what kind of shit.

"We have to work together, Chase."

Right. Against one of the most vicious gangs in the country. He caught sight of her pretty pink toenails peeking out from under her blanket. Him and the pretty little small town teacher up against Raphael Tessier. Maybe the bad guys would die laughing.

He meant to back away. To leave. Before her clean scent began absorbing into his skin. But with Lily, things never quite worked out the way he planned. Good intention turned into forward movement. Until they were chest-to-chest and hip-to-hip.

"Chase, be reasonable."

Reasonable? He could smell her. Her breasts pressed against his chest with every breath. He'd left reasonable so far behind he'd need a map to find it.

Then it was too late anyway. He needed to know if she tasted the same. Felt the same. And she was right there. In front of him. All he had to do was bend his head. Just a fraction of a movement and his self-imposed exile would end.

And he was only human.

So he tipped his head and put his mouth on hers. Ran the tip of his tongue over her bottom lip and got a yes to question number one.

His hands did a slow glide up her arms, over her shoulders to her face. He gently tilted her head and waited. Waited for the slight parting of her lips, the invitation to enter. When it came, it almost brought him to his knees.

He dove in like a man who'd been too long in the desert and she was his first taste of water in years. He needed his tongue in her mouth, tasting, savoring. He needed the warmth pulsing through his system to burn forever.

He broke contact with the thought of getting closer and realized he had her pushed up against the wall. Ugly flashbacks of his mother sandwiched between his father and a wall like the one holding them up shot through him. There'd been bruises on her, too. Put there by a man who claimed to love her more than life.

He squeezed his eyes shut and willed the image away. He knew he wasn't the man his father had been, but why tempt fate, not with the one woman who made him feel too much, too fast.

"I'm sorry." He put a hand over her fingers still gripping his shirt and tugged them free. One step back, two steps back, three steps back. Distance might not be a miracle cure, but it took the edge off his craving to stay. "I should go."

He headed for the door and left her standing there, stunned confusion showing on her pale face. Her fuzzy blue blanket pooled on the floor at her feet.

Chapter Six

One bleary eye squinted open, then another. The ding dong of her doorbell sounded again. She glared at her alarm clock and the huge red numbers showing beyond a doubt it was barely eight o'clock in the morning. On a Saturday. She'd managed a grand total of three hours sleep. Five long hours short of the perfect amount.

The aggravating dinging started up again. She burrowed down into her warm sheets and yanked the comforter up over her head despite the early morning heat. It stopped. The pounding began. She threw off her comfy covers, marched into her bathroom and came back out—teeth clenched, mangling her lightweight summer robe—ready to go to war.

Because, oh no, he wouldn't dare. Not even he possessed the amount of nerve needed. She fought through the folds of her robe, punched her arms into the sleeves, belting it in place.

Only Chase Porter would be stupid enough to show up at her front door this early in the morning after kissing her brains loose the night before and bolting for the door two seconds later. She ran her tongue over her lips, remembered the taste of him, the feel, and most importantly, the view of his back on his way out. The coward.

Even an idiot of gigantic proportions knew last night's exit came with a never-come-back proviso.

Some things were a given.

She stomped to the door and flung it open. "What?"

"I get that you're mad, but considering the current situation, you should really ask for a visitor's identification before opening the door."

If only one could neuter with a single thought. She growled and heaved the door shut. The man gave new meaning to the words "death" and "wish."

More knocking stopped her mid stride. A muffled "Come on, Lily" sounded through the wood. She retraced her steps. She opened the door for a second time. Why? Because she needed her head examined. Possibly other parts of her as well. Unmentionable parts. Take her vagina, for instance, which had shot out of hibernation mode straight into crazy, hot, needy mode because of a kiss.

"In case it's escaped your notice, I'm not in the mood to entertain." *Bonehead.*

"I just need a minute. To say I'm sorry. About last night. I was out of line. It won't happen again. Peace offering?" He held out a little box with a couple of takeout coffees and two muffins. Which might have been appealing if he looked the least bit sorry or pleading or hangdog, but he didn't. He looked stoic. Resigned.

The coffee smelled divine. Not him. The coffee. The sight of him did nothing for her. She had rendered herself immune, especially against faded denim jeans, snug black T-shirts and motorcycle boots.

Yes, she had.

For all eternity.

"Really?" She crossed her arms. "Does this apology cover the multiple times you were out of line, or one specific one?"

"Very funny." He lips flat lined. "Maybe we could discuss this somewhere other than your front door?"

She hugged herself tighter and watched his eyes fall to her chest and stick there, which reminded her of what she was wearing—very little. A miniscule ripple of something flashed through her system, a teeny snap of power. It cattle prodded her sense of revenge into action and prompted someone, who sounded a lot like Lily Wheeler, to say, "Why not. Come on in." And someone who felt a lot like Lily Wheeler backed up.

He hesitated, which proved he still owned two functioning brain cells, then stepped over her threshold like the proverbial fly. She let her arms drop along with her inhibitions.

"You know the way." Her robe parted as her hands went to her waist. She presented him with an eyeful of cleavage and a sliver of skin all the way to her navel. She often slept naked. It was the only decadent, sensual thing she indulged in. Seeing his eyes darken and the little tic develop along his jaw line was the cherry on the top of her personal ice cream sundae.

"I can wait while you put some clothes on."

"That's okay, I'm fine." And, for the first time in days, she was more than fine. She was on a roll. She ran the tip of her tongue along her top lip. "Would you like me to take that? It smells heavenly."

He narrowed his eyes in suspicion but with something else, too. That little something went a long way in soothing her battered confidence.

He put a hand out in the direction of her kitchen. "I've got it. You lead the way."

She sashayed into her tiny kitchen and, in supreme artistic fashion, arranged herself against the cupboards. Motioned for him to put his peace offering down beside her.

"You're not wearing much under that robe are you?" He dropped the box onto the counter. A whiff of coffee rose into the air.

She inhaled and expanded her chest. "That doesn't bother you, does it? Because you're not interested. Remember?"

"I didn't say I wasn't interested."

She nodded. "That's right. You said you were sorry." She held up a finger. "And that you had to go. Silly of me to misinterpret that."

He yanked a hand through his hair. "You're playing with fire here, Lily."

She smiled, picked up her coffee, and brought it to her lips. "I'm playing with something."

"Then don't blame me when we both get burnt." He stood stockstill, not moving a muscle, coiled. Ready to act or to retreat?

"That's not likely to happen. Is it? Because you've got it all figured out? Without having been around for a decade, you show up and designate yourself as my watchdog." She sipped her warm, strong coffee.

"Is it so wrong? To not want to see you get hurt." There was a glimpse of something there, but she ignored it and concentrated on setting him straight.

"Only if you refuse to sit or stop on command." She allowed a little smile to lift the corner of her lips as she set her cup down.

"Careful." His muscles uncoiled a smidge.

"Hurt how? By whom?" She searched his eyes, gave a tug on her robe. "By this man, Raphael Tessier? Or by you? Who are you protecting me from? Because last night wasn't about saving me from Raphael Tessier."

"What if it's both?" His gaze slipped downward.

"Then that's not okay. Fine, do your job. Deal with the gang situation. Protect Jason." She braced her hands on the counter, causing a further gape in her lapels. "But I'm a big girl and I don't need or like you making my decisions for me."

A muscle worked long his jaw, and his Adam's

apple started to bob. "What is it you want me to say?"

"I want you to be honest with me."

"Honest?" His laugh shattered the quiet of the kitchen.

"Yes, honest. I deserve honest from you." Her fingers clenched around the edges of her robe. She forgot seductive, she forgot smart. He was the only thing she saw, and the only thing she felt was ten years of separation.

"You have no idea. The things I want to do to you." He leaned in, rested his hands on the countertop, trapping her. "How much I want to strip you down. How much I want to take and take and take." When she tried to turn away, he grabbed her chin. "Oh no, you don't. You wanted it. Deal with it."

She swallowed, or at least, she tried. She suspected all her saliva had evaporated as she heated up from the inside out. Her skin pebbled up, and her nipples sharpened into little needy points.

"Hard, fast, and anywhere I can get it. How's that for the truth?"

He softened his touch, stroked a hand across her cheek, and brushed his hips against hers, leaving no doubt he spoke the truth. "I'm not your white picket fence type of guy. I'm not your type. I have no plans to stay. But I'm walking a fine line here, Lily. Between doing what I know is right and taking what I want. So give the femme fatale act a rest."

She hesitated. For once, she didn't want to do the right thing. The sensible thing. The good girl thing.

"As for Tessier...I'm going to feast on every second of payback that bastard has coming for putting his hands on you."

Rebel thoughts whispered through her mind, like a breeze swirling up the fallen autumn leaves.

Want it.

Try it.

She risked a glance into those familiar eyes in a stranger's face. A face molded and sharpened by experience, angles replaced the roundness of youth, giving testimony to the things he'd seen and no doubt done. It eclipsed the boy he'd been, marked the man he'd become.

Take it.

She lifted up onto her tiptoes and placed her lips on his unyielding ones. Her hands slid up his arms and over his stiff shoulders. He didn't budge. She coaxed with her tongue, ran her hands up his neck, and slowly slid them into his hair. He tugged on her arms, and the pressure forced her hands to slip loose. Powered by recklessness, she bit his bottom lip.

And unleashed a storm.

One with enough power to capsize her. An experienced sailor might have managed to keep afloat, but she started to drown the moment his tongue plunged into her mouth. Desire swept her away. He yanked her close, and the only life preserver she had was a thin, thigh length cotton robe. Not that she cared.

His hands shot into her hair, gripping her head, holding it in place while his talented tongue did incredible things inside her mouth. He pumped out heat like a bonfire and she was the marshmallow speared on the end of the roasting stick. The heat had her insides going gooey and the rest of her going up in flames.

The ringing sound confused her, until she realized it was the phone.

"Leave it." It was one demand she could live with, especially considering he'd moaned it against her lips.

Yes, leave it for her answering machine.

"Lily, it's me, Mike."

Mike? Who she hadn't heard from last night, Mike?

She scrambled to pull away and pick up the handset, fumbled it in her urge to hurry, and caught it again with no help at all from Chase who growled.

"Mike, it's me." She shut her eyes and tried not to sound out of breath, or nearly naked. Chase backed up a whole millimeter. She gave up trying to pull the edges of her robe together.

"I don't want you to worry, okay?"

"Okay." Warning bells clanged. She gripped the phone hard enough to cause a slight creak in protest.

"We haven't managed to find Jason."

"What?" She shoved hard enough on Chase's chest to send him back a step.

"I need your help. For ideas and some alternate places to look?"

"Of course, I'll help. I'll be right there." She pushed the phone at Chase and ran for her bedroom to the words, "Mike, what the hell?"

****

His pants were too tight, what with having to house the counterproductive powers of his junk and his brains in the same place. The seat groaned as he shifted behind the wheel of his truck, trying in vain to get comfortable. They were traveling to the detachment in separate vehicles. Her idea, not his. He gave another useless pull at the material hugging his crotch. She'd gotten him so twisted up he didn't know if he was coming or going.

If he had his pick?

Coming, definitely coming.

He snorted. Right. Like that wouldn't be the worst damn decision ever. His hormones needed to suck it up. Sex with Lily? Not happening. Except in his dreams, where it played out in slow motion torture and high definition sensation. Every night. Those futile nighttime conjuring's jacked him full of ideas. Ideas he hung out to dry and fry in the sun. Until now.

He flashed back to the kitchen. Big mistake. He shifted again. He wanted back there so bad he could taste it. Taste her. Taste them.

Everything deflated when he pulled into the parking lot of the police station, his erection and his good intentions. Keep it simple sounded manageable in the early morning hours with his brain in charge, but the moment his cock took over, it acted like a compass pointing North. And go figure, his north would be Lily.

Lily leaped out of her vehicle before he could get to her and help her out, no doubt anxious to get to Mike. Mike, who waited to buzz them into the building. Mike, who was all eager beaver. The same Mike who should be telling her to stay out of the way.

Mike laid a hand on Lily's arm, and Chase's fingers twitched. "Can I get you guys a coffee? Anything?"

Chase declined and shrugged off Mike's what-the-hell-are-you-doing-here look. Besides, the very last thing he needed was coffee. Unless it contained whiskey. Or a reality check. Anything to give him an edge of perspective.

Mike shrugged, picked up a file, and headed toward the interrogation room.

Chase caught sight of the faint flush of red appearing at the base of Lily's throat before she trailed after Mike. It went a long way to alleviating his mood. Until the rest of him noticed, too. He cleared his throat and shoved his hands in his front pockets. Resolutions and priorities pushed back into place, he tracked Lily and Mike down in the interrogation room.

Once inside the tiny room, he went over his options. Or rather option. Get her in and get her out.

Then Mike opened his mouth.

"First off, let me say I'm not overly worried. There's no evidence anything's happened. But I want to locate him." Once again, Mike reached out and put a hand on Lily's arm. Chase's good idea-bad idea scale nose-dived in the wrong direction. Mike continued on, "If you could provide us with a list of friends and places to look that would be great."

Mike laid a paper and pen down on the cold metal table and pulled out a chair for Lily. Lily sank into it. Mike claimed the one next to her. Chase gritted his teeth as he made his way to the opposite side of the table.

"Have you found out anything else?" The hopefulness in her voice stabbed him in the chest.

"Not much, no." Mike leaned in as Lily stiffened.

"Yet?" The years between then and now hadn't diminished her glass-is-half-full tendencies.

Mike reached out a hand, squeezed Lily's shoulder, and smiled. "Yet."

All the touching, the smiles, the inclusion of Lily in a process Chase considered way too dangerous, not to mention confidential, caused a bunch of something dark to work its way up from his center. Time to bring a dose of reality to the tea party. "He knows something. Something big."

"Agreed." Mike handed the file to Chase.

Chase flipped through the first few pages. Nothing new or earth shattering shot off the page. He finished skimming, closed the file, and placed it very carefully to his right, out of her reach. Her hands went to her lap, and her lashes slipped down to cover her reaction, but not before he saw her irises flash.

He stripped everything personal from his tone. "What do you know about Jason's brother, Kevin?"

A little furrow of concentration plowed across her forehead as she paused for a moment to think about her answer. "Next to nothing. He's, what, four or five years older than Jason? Before my time teaching here. I know he's been in trouble with the police, but that's it."

"Does Jason talk about him? Have you seen him around?"

"Not to me. And no."

He exchanged another silent message with Mike.

"Have you ever suspected Jason of using drugs?"

"What? No!" Genuine shock parted her lips and widened her eyes. Still, teachers didn't know every damn thing.

"You're absolutely positive?" He pushed because Kevin McCarran had several drug possession convictions. The Prairie Brotherhood was a major drug supplier to the Prairie Provinces. The dots were random, scattered, but they still needed to connect.

Her pretty eyes narrowed. "Why? What are you not telling me?"

He leaned forward, rested his elbows on the table. Stalled for a second while he shifted through which details to reveal. "We're looking for a link. A connection."

"Between Jason and the Prairie Brotherhood." She switched her attention to Mike. "And you think Kevin McCarran is it? Do you think he's forcing Jason to join his gang?"

Mike shook his head. "I'd have to say no. I don't have as much experience as Chase, but I'd say no. Gangs are definitely making their presence known in this part of the province, but their recruitment initiatives run more to persuasion tactics. This feels different."

Chase agreed. "Recruitment doesn't typically work that way, not that it can't, but it doesn't usually. There is a procedure involved in joining a gang. 'Recruits' generally need a sponsor who is a confirmed gang member, someone who will vouch for their loyalty. A lot of recruiting also goes on in correctional facilities."

It didn't require much brainpower to make the leap. She made it in the snap of a finger. "And Kevin McCarran spent time in jail?"

He nodded. Imagined the wheels spinning inside her gorgeous head. He wasn't disappointed.

"Where's Kevin McCarran now?" she asked.

"That's the sixty-four thousand dollar question. Up until six months ago, Kevin McCarran had shared a cell with a top-ranking member of the Prairie Brotherhood. In fact, half the cellblock read like a who's who of the Brotherhood criminal organization."

"But you don't know where he is now?"

"We need to talk to Jason. To see if he's been in contact."

"I can help you get the answers you need. I can try talking to Jason again. I can—"

"Lily, this is a police investigation. Your involvement can only go so far." Mike reached for the file.

Chase stepped in before Lily could open her mouth to protest. He aimed for reasonable, professional, but wanted to leave no mistake as to his purpose or his intent. "Jason is not the only one who needs our protection. You need to be added to the list."

"Oh, enough with the protectionist attitude. I don't need—"

"Yes, you do. Until you have a clear understanding of what these people are capable of, until you are ready to take this threat seriously, you do need precautionary protection. Do not delude yourself into thinking these men are honorable or principled in any way."

She jabbed a finger at her chest. "So now I'm

delusional? I was there. Remember? I know what they're capable of."

"We don't think you're delusional," said Mike. He shot a warning look at Chase. "You want to help Jason, that's admirable. We appreciate it. However, it would help us if your involvement tended toward a more advisory capacity with no direct connection outside of school."

"I can handle it, Mike."

Chase doubted it. Against the washed out walls, the harsh lines of the small room, she appeared too fragile by half. "Before you decide if you can 'handle' it or not, let's get one thing straight. These men are soldiers following orders from their general. The men who attacked you do not have the option of failing. They will do whatever it takes to get the job done."

Again she chose to turn to the man sitting beside her. "Mike, you know me. You know I can help." She kept her eyes on Mike, leaving Chase with no doubt in his mind regarding her preference. His skin heated and his brain contracted. Damn this town. Damn her, for making a tough job unbearable.

"Chase has a point. You've never dealt with people like this." Finally, some reason.

"But I do deal with teenagers, of which Jason is one. I see him five days a week. Let me help."

"Lily." said Mike.

Over his dead or dying body.

"Please, Mike." That please should have been his. From her lips to his ears.

It was the last straw. Chase pushed out of his chair, sent it screeching backward. Lily flinched, which he hated and regretted. It didn't stop him.

"You think I'm exaggerating?"

"Chase." Mike's tone contained a truckload of forewarning.

Chase shook his head at Mike. "No, she needs to

know who she's dealing with. I'm not blowing smoke out my ass when I say these people are dangerous."

"You're acting like I'm going to go out and hunt down gang bangers. I assure you, I am not." She pushed back a cluster of curls. Her eyes, the heat in them, turned him to stone.

"And yet you've been in contact with them. Twice."

"Not intentionally." But her gaze shifted away from his.

"Really? You just happened to be running errands in Jason's neighborhood yesterday?"

"I wasn't aware it was a crime to worry about someone." Her eyes were back on his, branding him.

"You intentionally put yourself in harm's way." He refused to let it go. Understanding the seriousness of their situation was paramount to keeping her, and everyone else, safe. He was fully prepared to figuratively shove the facts down her slim throat

"That's your view of the day's events." She crossed her arms over her chest.

Mike intervened. "All we're asking is that you come to us first with any information you might get and not to enter into any confrontation with them again."

"Thank you, Mike." But she aimed it at Chase. "I appreciate your support."

"We'll keep in touch and let you know how best to help." Mike picked up the file signaling an end to the meeting.

"Start by replacing your phone and next time, don't get out of the damn car." Chase lost reasonable, skipped over subtle, and refused to be affected by her pale face with the too prominent freckles, damn it.

She jerked out of her chair and pointed a finger at him. "You are insufferable, you know that? Don't believe, even for one second, you can waltz back into town and start ordering me around."

He stared straight into those wide, blue eyes, made the connection they were both intent on ignoring. "You're in trouble. I'm a cop. It is my job."

Mike closed his eyes and rubbed his forehead. Chase couldn't have cared less. He was justified in his reasoning. And terrified. He didn't have to explain why.

"Congratulations to you. Tell me, is this Neanderthal type behavior a requirement for members of law enforcement everywhere or a little something extra you picked up along the way to charm the masses?"

The laugh he let loose into the room didn't encourage reciprocation. "My behavior is going to keep you, and the kid you're so fond of, alive."

"Could you be any more conceited?" At the disbelieving shake of her head, every muscle tightened, and a flush heated his neck.

"What I am is good at my job."

"This may come as a shock, but I'm equally adept at mine."

Mike sighed. "Children, could we please play nice?"

Chase shoved his hands through his hair and ignored him. "Let me ask you this. Who's in charge of your classroom, Lily?" He let a couple seconds pass before continuing. "You are. How else would you maintain order?"

Qualifying for the biggest asshole of the year award might give him chest pains, but it didn't stop him. He had her, and she knew it, but he wasn't finished. "And here's another thing. How are you going to feel if Jason gets hurt because of you?"

"That's a low blow." She wrapped her arms around her stomach like she was in pain, but she still had the guts to meet him eye to eye. "I would never forgive myself if something happened to him because of me."

Mike walked up and put his hands on her shoulders and cut Chase off. "Lily, I know you would never do anything to hurt Jason. It would help us out if you kept an eye on him in school, monitor how he's doing. If he wants to open up to you, great. But don't approach the Prairie Brotherhood on your own and, above all, don't underestimate them."

She patted Mike's hand. "I won't." Something changed in her tone. Chase couldn't quite put his finger on it, but it made the hair on the back of his neck stand up. She lifted her chin. "Well, we'd better get started."

His eyes narrowed and a bad feeling raked claws up his spine. "Started on what?"

"On looking."

"*We'll* get started on looking. You can go home."

"I don't think so, I'm coming with you." A smug smile tipped the corner of her lips.

"Oh, no, you're not."

"Yes. I am." She widened her smile, and the temperature in the room dropped ten degrees. "You don't know his friends, you don't know the people, and you don't know where to go to look."

"I don't think—"

"I don't know about—"

She held up a hand, silencing them both. "I will be going with someone."

Mike, the coward, recovered the quickest. "On second thought, it's an excellent idea."

Imparting reason was like trying to climb upward during a rockslide. Chase tried anyway. "Since when do civilians accompany us on the job?"

Mike punched him lightly on the arm. "Since you're not officially on the job until Monday, and since all you're doing is scouting things out, I don't see any harm in it. I'll run it by Jeff. It'll be fine.

Leave a list of places to check out on my desk. Have fun." He paused, halting his world record sprint to the door. "And good luck."

Lily crossed her arms, raised an eyebrow, and scored a point. "You can always call it precautionary protection."

****

They completed the short walk to his truck in silence. Smugness rolled off her to mix and mingle with the late summer heat. It was in the lift of her chin, her barely-there smile, her stride. Chase waited while Lily climbed in and buckled up. He shut her door and made his way to the driver's side. Kept his cool as he settled in behind the wheel. He hated being out maneuvered.

"Let's get one thing straight." Or a hundred things.

"Fine." Her tone set his teeth on edge. He spied her accompanying eye roll and crushed another molar to dust. Like he was the irrational one. When the opposite was fact.

"Under no circumstances are you to leave this truck unless I give you permission. If you so much as put a toe on the running board without my say so, I will haul your delectable ass back home, no matter what your good friend *Mike* or my boss says. Understood?"

"Perhaps a good place to start would include you putting a lid on your sewer mouth."

"How about we start with finding a secluded spot so my sewer mouth can become intimately acquainted with your delectable ass, along with the rest of you."

She gave him the you-are-such-a-juvenile look. "You can be as disgusting as you want, I'm coming with you. And you can threaten to take me home all you want, but we both know that's not going to happen."

"I swear to—"

"Ah, ah, ah. No swearing, remember."

"This is my truck and I'll swear if I want."

"No. You won't." She glanced down at the list in her hands and back up. "We're wasting time. I think the first place we should look is west of the tracks. That little wooded area behind Logan's Lumberyard."

"Why would we look there?" Like he didn't know.

"Because it's where you used to hide, remember?"

Only when forced. "I could have found that place on my own."

"Yes, but you wouldn't have thought of looking there on your own."

He ground his teeth together and swore he heard another tooth crack. The faster they ripped through the stupid list the better. "Why do you think he might be there?"

"I don't know, call it female intuition."

"Great." He wanted to call it bat shit crazy but he wasn't allowed to swear in his own truck. He threw the truck into reverse. At this rate, one of them wasn't coming back alive. Odds suggested it might be him.

She sighed.

He gripped the wheel.

She sighed again.

Do. Not. Ask.

"You're being ridiculous, you know."

Hell. On. Earth. It had to be. Where else would he find himself stuck in a confined space with someone who looked and smelled like candy coated chocolate and thought like a Rottweiler?

"And unreasonable."

"If by unreasonable you mean right, then, yes I am."

"Turn left here."

"I know where to turn."

"See what I mean."

Someone shoot him. He knew from firsthand experience it was less painful. "So besides 'female intuition' do you have any other reasons why he might be hiding in the woods?"

"Not really. But it's a small town and there aren't that many places to hide. So, I've been trying to think of any abandoned buildings, that kind of thing."

Her idea made sense, and it stung. Hell, he should have thought of it. Would have thought of it if lust and rational thinking made a compatible combination. "Okay, we'll give it a shot."

His old hideout in the woods was a bust. No sign of recent habitation, nothing but tall grass, wild bush, and bad memories. "Any other ideas?"

"One or two. There's an old house, you might remember it, used to be the Danforth place. It's close enough to town without being in town. It's empty, has been for a while."

"I remember it." Without thinking he offered a smile and held out a hand to her like he had numerous times in this same spot. "Come on, let's go check it out."

She paused for a couple of seconds. Her thought patterns played across her face. He kept his hand out anyway. She ignored his offer and his hand. Instead, she walked past him to climb into his truck. He swiped his hand through a patch of thigh high grass. Message received.

Except for directions, they drove to the Danforth place in silence. A silence that snaked its way around the cab of his truck and knotted itself around each of them, ensuring they remained separate and apart. He stared straight ahead while she directed her attention out the passenger window.

By the time they'd pulled up to their second destination, a wall was forming, brick by stubborn brick. He should have been grateful.

"Here we are." He put the truck into park and dipped his head down to get a better look at the deserted house. "This house is the exact reason I preferred the woods. Place gives me the creeps. I mean, why trade one nightmare for another?" He felt her eyes swing toward him and, too late, he remembered he'd vowed to give nothing away.

"Chase…"

He shrugged and slapped some mortar on their invisible wall and placed another imaginary brick. "It was a long time ago." He didn't want what was between them, or what she was feeling, to be about tenderness or sympathy.

He climbed out of the truck and waited for her to do the same.

They scoured every inch of the broken down, dilapidated, sagging two-story house and found nothing. The only evidence of habitation was the traces left behind by rats and other rodents. He could hear them in the walls and under the floorboards.

Lily rubbed her arms. "Let's get out of here. I've never been so thankful not to find someone."

Once on the porch, he jumped down over the broken steps and held out his hands. "Time for lunch, I'm starving."

She eyed his hands.

"Chicken," he goaded.

"I am not a chicken. I'm fully capable of getting down on my own. I did manage to climb up, after all."

"Like I said, chicken."

"Now you're being silly." Hands on hips, she faced him down.

He whistled through his teeth. "I think you've

got that a bit turned around."

"I'm not the one squawking."

"Scared of getting your hands dirty?" The thought came out of the blue. That it was unwarranted and irrelevant didn't matter. He said it to wound, and it worked.

"That's not it, and you know it." The truth of it flashed in her eyes, showed in her hands as they slid from her hips.

"Prove it." He said it to be perverse. He wanted her hands on his skin, and he wanted her to want it, too. As badly as he did. The life or death need all but choked off his air supply.

"I would, if I had anything to prove, but I don't."

"But I do." He acted without thinking, and it cost him. In two seconds flat, she was squirming around in his arms like a wild barn cat, parts of her rubbing against parts of him. Warm, soft, and smelling like a full-bodied prairie wind and the ripening harvest.

"I'm going to drop you if you don't stop wiggling." He pretended to let go, and her hands grabbed for his neck.

"You—"

"Careful, no swearing, remember?" And he laughed because he had her exactly where he wanted her, speechless and clinging to him.

Her chest heaved, her nostrils flared—incensed, she was magnificent.

"Cretin. Put me down. Right now."

He couldn't help it, he laughed again.

Her blue eyes flamed. "Jerk. Idiot."

"Come on, you can do better than that." But he set her down anyway. Careful to let his hands trail over as much of her as possible. She looked past him, refused to meet his gaze. He felt her entire body tighten, close off, and he shut his eyes.

He was such a fool.

Chapter Seven

Lily's body stiffened against the onslaught of feeling, from the complications of a desire spring boarding its way past the shallow end of sanity, straight into a deep pool of lust gone wrong. She shut her eyes against the inevitable drowning. She pried them open again in time to catch Jason rounding the corner of the house. She froze. Blinked again.

"Jason."

They'd found him. The wave of relief stilled her fingers, her heart, and redirected her misguided intentions back to what mattered.

At the sight of them, Jason skittered to a halt. The wild prairie grass whipped at his thin legs as the shock pushed him back a step, slackened his jaw. Two seconds later, he bolted back in the opposite direction.

She stumbled back when Chase released her to jerk around and face the commotion.

"Jason, wait!" She grabbed for Chase's arm. "If he makes the tree line at the back of the property he's gone."

"I've got him."

He sprinted after Jason, his long legs eating up the distance. Chase gained the corner of the ancient two-story house seconds after Jason disappeared around it.

A sudden whiff of wind sent shivers through the

long grass. She forced her legs into a dash for the corner, which she rounded in time to see Chase gaining ground on Jason, who she was signing up for the track and field team as soon as possible. Chase tackled him ten feet from the tree line.

Her hand flew to her mouth as they stumbled and went down. She forced a bit more speed out of her legs and headed for the mad scramble and the noise.

"Let me go." Jason rushed to get up, all elbows and knees. He didn't get very far.

Chase grunted. "Take it easy. We just want to talk to you." But as soon as he was upright, Jason tried to run again.

"Son of a—" Chase reached out, grabbed hold of Jason's arm and pulled him back. "Hold it right there."

She bent over, hands to knees, as she sucked in air.

Jason struggled to break free. If the resounding "Ouch" was anything to go by, he'd managed to connect something of his with something vital of Chase's.

"I think you can let him go now." She shoved a mass of annoying curls out of her eyes and speared Jason with her best teacher stare. "He won't try and run again. Will you?"

Jason ripped his arm out of Chase's grasp and backed up a step. She put a cautionary hand on Chase's arm.

"We just want to make sure you're all right." It was the truth, but he clearly didn't trust them. He still had bolting at the first opportunity written all over him.

"I'm fine. Or I was before he went all crazy on me."

"Jason, things are not fine."

Jason glared in her direction. "Who is he,

anyway?"

Chase interrupted. "I'm the guy trying to get you out of trouble. So show some respect."

"Bite me."

"Okay, let's all take a minute to calm down." She pointed a finger at Jason. "Not another inch."

"I got nothing to say." Mutinous didn't even begin to describe him.

"Let us be the judge of that. Could be you know more than you think." Chase swiped hands over his shirt and jeans, sending wisps of grass and leaves into the air.

She tried for a consolatory tone. "What have you got to lose? You can't like hiding out in the woods."

"Besides, you've got more to offer than information."

That got his attention. Jason sneered at Chase with the look of someone eyeing up a guy in a trench coat selling designer watches for ten bucks apiece. "Like what?"

Chase didn't appear deterred. "Like an introduction. Names. These men who are after you, they're members of a gang called the Prairie Brotherhood. I need to talk to them."

"Why?"

"Because they're involved in some very bad stuff."

"So, you're like a cop?" The left corner of Jason's lip lifted.

"Yes, I am."

"Sorry, can't help you."

"Jason, a little cooperation could go a long way in keeping you safe."

"I can look after myself."

"Yeah, right." Chase lifted up a strap of Jason's backpack, causing him to flinch. Jason grabbed on with both hands to hold it in place. "By hiding out in the woods or abandoned buildings?"

"Maybe I'm out for a hike."

Chase let go and Jason shifted the pack so it was out of Chase's reach.

"Want me to guess what's in the pack? A shirt, maybe another pair of jeans, all the money you've managed to scrounge, save, and keep hidden from your old man, who's not above stealing from you when he's desperate for booze money, a couple granola bars if you're lucky, and something—like a picture, a figurine, a piece of jewelry—something of your mom's."

Lily clamped down on her senses. Oh, sweet Heaven above, there was no going back now. She wanted to press her hand to her heart, to hold it in place. To hold it still. Her Chase, he was there, inside this other Chase. The boy who'd taken her heart, laid hands on her, taught her things. Wonderful things.

"How'd I do? Pretty close, huh?" Chase's stoic expression locked back in place.

Jason clamped his lips together in a rebellious line and looked past Chase toward the trees, refusing to acknowledge his guess.

"I know that because it's the same stuff I kept ready for the times I needed to move fast. Except for the money, I kept that hidden in the floor register. That and a picture of my mom."

Lily winced. Not once, during all the time they'd spent together, had he revealed this much about his life with his dad. Or how much he'd missed his mom. She hadn't known. Had she asked? Or just assumed too much? It was a demoralizing revelation.

Jason scoffed. "I'm supposed to believe that?"

Chase lifted a shoulder. "Don't take my word for it. Ask around. Ask the old timers. I bet they remember my dad, and what a mean drunk he could be."

Lily couldn't decide if she wanted to hug

someone, or if she wanted someone to hug her. Her heart broke listening to him, watching Jason listen to him. She caught the fleeting twinges of denial and hope warring against each other on his teenage face. She knew what it cost Chase to talk about his father. That he'd offered a glimpse to help a child, as cliché as it sounded, it made her weak in the knees.

What the heck was she going to do with weak knees?

"Fine. It doesn't change the fact that I don't know anything."

"Maybe the ride home will jar your memory."

"No way." If anything, Jason clutched tighter to his backpack.

She intervened, calm but firm. "We can drop you off at your aunt's."

"You can't make me go with you." He took a step back.

She reached out a hand. "We're not here to make you do anything."

Tires crunched across gravel in the distance. They all paused and looked back toward the house. Out of the corner of her eye, she saw Chase put a hand on Jason's shoulder. He didn't flinch, which showed her how vested he was in seeing who was going to walk around the corner of the house.

"Where's your other spot? Is it close?" Chase jostled his shoulder.

Jason glared up at Chase for a couple of seconds, then relented and nodded. "Douglas Road, the old Banton building."

"I'll meet you both there. Now go." Something passed between them, a connection, and with the sound of car doors slamming in the background, she forgot to care.

Jason headed for the trees and beckoned her to get a move on. To follow. Chase made tracks for the back of the house. She waved at Jason to run and darted after him, intent on keeping herself between Jason and whatever was coming.

They hustled into the woods, stopping on the other side of the tree line to check back. No sign of Chase. She braced herself against a tree.

"The Banton building?"

"Yeah."

"Let's go."

"Wait. We're going to leave him here?"

"I don't like it any better than you do. But our options appear to be limited."

"We can double back. There are trees or bush cover surrounding the whole place, almost to the front of the house."

"It doesn't make any difference." She wiped sweaty palms down the sides of her pants as she searched for a glimpse of Chase. "Besides, it's too dangerous."

She waited for Jason to answer, her concentration locked on the back of the house and the spot she'd last seen Chase. When no answer came, she glanced over her shoulder and saw nothing. Or rather, no one.

"Jason?" She hissed his name out as quietly as she could while staving off a full-blown panic attack. The sight of him dodging trees on his way back toward trouble sent her racing after him. The sprint through the trees put a tear in her favorite shirt, ripped out a chunk or two of hair, and cost her the rest of her wits. She only caught up to him because he stopped to rummage through his backpack.

"What are you doing? Come on, let's go." She grabbed his arm, but he shook her off.

"He was wrong about one thing." He dragged out a shirt and started unwinding it from around something. A second later, a shiny blade glinted in a patch of sunlight.

"Jason! Put that away." She backed up a step.

"I'm going to slash their tires." He grinned at her like it was the best plan on earth instead of the worst.

"What? Absolutely not."

"There are only two of them. One's in the house and one's around back."

"How do we even know they're the bad guys?"

"They had the right colors. One was carrying."

"Carrying what?" But she was very afraid she knew what.

"A gun." The duh was implied.

She stared at him. "What? There's no way you can know that for sure. This isn't a joke, Jason. You're not James Bond, and this isn't a movie set."

He frowned at her. "What?"

"Never mind. It's too risky. This isn't a game. You could get hurt or worse. Or we could end up getting Chase hurt." Not to mention what he was going to do to them when he found out they hadn't left.

"He can handle it."

She rolled her eyes at his tone, like all of a sudden he and Chase understood each other. Before she could stop him, he sprinted off in the direction of the two vehicles parked in front of the house.

She tried to keep her voice low. "Jason, get back here right now." He ignored her. She stomped her foot and screamed on the inside. He was in such big trouble. They both were if she didn't get them out of there. She bent over as low as she could get to the ground and sprinted after him.

The hiss of air greeted her when she crouched down by the back bumper of the late model black sedan. He was a fast worker, she'd give him that, but the knowledge did nothing to calm her down.

An angry shout sounded from the direction of the front of the house. She shut her eyes tight, and a strange tingling sensation, something akin to terror, overtook her limbs. Crap on a stick.

She started gesturing to get Jason's attention when a shout sounded from the porch.

"In the truck. Now." Chase's big black truck, parked next to the sedan, rumbled to life and the locks clicked open. Thank goodness for technology and remote car starters.

Neither of them wasted any time. They both dove in through the passenger door at the exact same time Chase clambered in the driver's side door. He jammed the keys into the ignition and gravel flew as he pushed the truck into gear and stomped on the gas.

"Get down!"

She grabbed onto the back of Jason's head and pushed him down. A shot sounded as they fishtailed down the lane. No glass shattered, no metal creaked or caved in, and she offered up a prayer of thanks.

"This is so sweet!" It was muffled, but it was hard to miss the excitement in Jason's voice.

"No, not sweet. Stupid. What the hell were you thinking, kid?" Chase dug out his cell phone and tossed it in her direction. "Call it in."

"Watch the language, please." She pushed herself up and rubbed a hand over her forehead before starting to press numbers.

"Dude, I totally saved your ass."

"Hey, both of you. Language!"

"*Dude,* I had everything under control. Hang on." But when Chase checked the rearview mirror, she saw his lips twitch. She looked back to see two men trying to beat their car to death. They swished around the corner onto a loose gravel road and she almost dropped the phone when Jason slid into her.

Finished with her call, she pressed *end* just as the truck fishtailed again. She dropped the phone and grabbed for something solid. A huge pothole in the road sent the whole truck skidding, spraying gravel in all directions. They bounced around the cab of the truck like bingo balls. She was going to have bruises on top of bruises.

"Now what?" Jason dropped his cool-and-detached in favor of let's-do-it-again.

"Now we go to the station and file a report."

"Ah, man."

"After that we'll figure out a safe place for you to stay."

She put a hand over her pounding heart. "I've had enough excitement for one day. Thanks. We need to get you somewhere safe." Then maybe, just maybe, she'd sleep tonight.

"Once that's settled I'm going to deal with Miss Wheeler."

"Me?"

"Yes, you."

She refused to engage in an argument. Not while Jason sat between them, head swiveling back and forth and looking like all he needed was the popcorn, and he'd be a happy camper.

****

Lily led Mike out onto her front steps and lifted her face up to catch the leftover heat from the setting sun. It didn't help. The bone deep chill remained. She rubbed her arms, wishing for a sweater.

She wondered where Chase was and why he'd sent an emissary. "So, he's with his aunt?"

"Yeah. It's the best we can do for now." Mike offered a reassuring smile. "He'll be fine. We'll make sure of it. We've stationed someone outside for tonight."

Lily sighed. "An elderly aunt? Not much of a barrier. But I've got a friend in Student Services. I'll set up a meeting for Monday. Talk to Jason's aunt. We'll see what we can do."

"Sounds good."

She smiled up at Mike and wondered, not for the first time, why he didn't do it for her. Gorgeous didn't do him justice. Blonde, green-eyed, and he had to top the growth chart at about six feet three inches. "Thanks for stopping by."

"No problem." He ran a hand up and down her arm. "Do me a favor? Tell Grace next time you talk to her, I stopped by her place to check on things while she's gone." He winked.

She laughed. "I'll do that. She's sure to be most impressed."

"Liar." He nudged her shoulder with one of his own and offered up a rueful glance. "Gotta go."

"I know." Lily put a hand to his back as she ushered him down the steps. At the sight of Chase stopped halfway up her walk, his eyes glued on Mike, she jerked to a stop. She forced her smile back into place.

"Good luck, beautiful." She caught Mike's whispered chuckle a second before his breath brushed against her cheek. Then he dropped a big smacking kiss on the same spot. Another chuckle and he headed down the walk.

Chase stepped back to watch Mike climb into his vehicle. Then his attention zeroed in on her.

She crossed her arms and waited for him to close the distance separating them, but he chose to stay rooted to his spot like an ornery thistle.

She tilted her head after the departing vehicle. "Mike stopped by to fill me in on a few details."

"That right?"

She rolled her eyes. "Yes. That's right."

"Then I don't need to bother." He turned to leave, and she realized Mike had come on his own. Chase hadn't sent him in his place.

"Wait." She stepped down onto the first step of the porch, hating what she was about to do, but powerless to stop it. "Do you want to come in? For a drink or something?" It sounded like a very bad come on. "You know, I could probably scrounge up a bite to eat, some ice tea?" Which sounded worse than desperate. It bordered on begging.

"I don't think so." He shoved his hands in his pockets and shrugged. "I should be going. 'Night, Lily."

So final. Like he'd made an earth shattering decision in the time it took her to blink. Turned some imaginary corner. She backed up, shut the front door on his departing back, bolted it shut, and banished herself to the backyard.

After going with Chase and Jason to the station, she'd taken her car into the local garage to have the passenger window replaced. No car plus no plans equaled too much time to think.

On her back deck, she stopped to cup a fragile bloom cascading over the edge of one of the many flowerpots scattered across her deck. She pinched off the flower, brought it to her nose, and inhaled the gentle fragrance. She risked a glance in the direction of Chase's house. Nothing to see. Trees blocked the beautiful two-story Victorian from view, but a surge of heat flashed under her skin at the images hypnotizing her. Her eyelids drifted shut as she trailed flower petals across her cheek, down the side of her neck—a soft substitute for the long, firm, callused fingers she pictured in its place.

Disgusted with herself, she tossed the pretty bloom to the ground. She seldom indulged in futile longings. And this one was not only futile, it was stupid. Crazy.

She wanted a white picket fence type guy. And he wasn't it. Hadn't he spelled out the fact this morning as she'd attempted her best Bettie Page all over her kitchen countertop? *Not staying,* he'd said. What she needed to do was move on. And she couldn't make that happen with Chase occupying space in her head. She had to find a way to dislodge him. Only she didn't have a clue how to start.

****

Lily jerked awake and sent the book resting on her stomach to the floor. Straining to focus, she blinked at her bedside clock. Midnight. Tired and cranky, she shut her eyes. Wished for sleep. It didn't work. On a sigh, she flipped off the covers, a drink of water and back to sleep. Hopefully straight through 'til morning.

Moonlight lit the way as she shuffled to the kitchen. Grabbing a glass, she opened the faucet. Her kitchen window overlooked her backyard, and she eyed herself in the dark glass. Mercy, she needed sleep. Bags were stacking themselves on top of each other under her eyes.

She stuck her tongue out at her reflection, then jerked back when something moved at the back of her tiny garden, disturbing the sunflowers she planted every spring. She pressed her face closer to the glass and let out a small shriek as someone sprinted through her tomatoes. She ducked down, hand over her mouth, holding in a scream. Someone was in her backyard.

Oh, crap. Oh, crap. Oh, crap.

Maybe she'd imagined it. It was possible. Who wouldn't after the last few days? She gripped the counter and hauled herself up, inch-by-inch, and peered through the glass.

Nothing.

Which didn't mean there hadn't been anything. Just that there was nothing there now. Or nothing visible to the naked eye in the dim moonlight except plenty of spots to hide. She dropped back down to the floor. She refused to go all hysterical and call in the troops over nothing. The whole town would know about it by morning.

Which left one option. She slapped a hand up

and around on the countertop in the last place she'd left the phone. Her fingers latched on and she stuck it in front of her face, paused, knocked the useless thing against her head. She didn't have his number. Why would she have his number? She shouldn't need Chase's number.

From her vantage point on the floor by the patio doors, she watched a shadow flit across her deck. She squeaked and then scrambled on all fours for the front door. She had enough sense to snatch up a blanket from her living room and wrap it around her midsection. The twenty second dash to Chase's house spanned hours worth of fretful glances back over her shoulder. She tripped up his front steps, her blanket in league with the devil.

No porch light to relieve her anxiety. Total and utter darkness. She pounded on the door and hugged her security blanket tight to her rolling stomach. The porch light snapped on, and she blinked.

"Lily? What is it? Is something wrong?"

No, she was standing out here in her panties and a tank top wrapped in a blanket for fun. "Someone's in my backyard." Her teeth chattered over the words.

"What?"

Was he deaf? "Someone—"

"Get in here."

"Gladly."

He grabbed her hand and hauled her through to his front room. He let go of her, but continued on through to the kitchen and came back with a flashlight. Something else disappeared behind his back.

"Stay here." He rearranged his shirt and headed for the door.

What? No. "Shouldn't I come with you?"

"No. Stay put." He left her standing in the middle of his living room. She eyed the huge flat screen television showing some action movie, let out a breath, and immediately sucked it in again. What the heck was that? The sound scraped over her frayed nerve endings again. She chalked it up to imagination. Until it happened again. Another long rasping creak. Her eyes slid right, toward the empty kitchen, the uncovered open window, the backdoor. Did the handle just rattle? All shadows. Her eyes shifted left. Three doors—closet, basement, Chase. She chose door number three.

She gathered the corners of her blanket closer together and raced for the door. For Chase.

"Ow." She slapped a hand over her mouth. She continued to hobble forward an inch at a time until she was forced to stop and clutch at the poplar tree edging his yard for support. She bent down to brush off the bottom of her bare foot. Stupid stones. The streetlight blinked once and went out.

Huh?

Dark. Very dark. And quiet. New plan. No, stick with the old one. Find Chase. Find anyone. Except the bad guy. She didn't want to find him.

Limping to save her injured foot, she picked her away around their shared hedge and mapped a track along the side of her house, hand over hand, to her back gate which she eased open, or tried to, before a twig snapped and caused a terror spasm. The clang of the catching latch echoed in the quiet as she froze in place. The path leading to the back corner of her house went a bit fuzzy.

A hand snaked out and covered her mouth. The other arm wrapped around her waist and yanked her close. Her back hit someone.

"Don't you ever stay where you're put?"

She stuttered into his rough palm, and he let her go.

"Shhh."

"Never scare me like that again."

Muttering a curse, he wedged himself in front of her face. “Stay right behind me, do not say a word, do not utter a sound, in fact—do not breathe, or so help me, I will duct tape you to something next time.”

She kept her mouth shut as ordered.

“Understand?”

“Just following orders.”

“Try again. The right answer this time.”

“Fine. Understood.”

He bared his teeth as he wagged a finger in her face. “Stay behind me.”

They covered every inch of the backyard and the front yard before moving into her house. He also checked every inch of the house, because she’d left her front door wide open. Which put him in a huff and left her relegated to a lounge chair on the back deck for the duration of the search.

Back in her kitchen, he ran a hand through his hair. “Nothing.”

“Well, thanks for looking anyway.”

“No problem.” He headed for the door.

She was so not ready to be left alone yet. “At least, let me make you coffee. I’ve got decaf.”

How asinine was that? Did he act like he drank decaf?

“I don’t think so.” But he didn’t move.

“Please. Don’t go.” She winced at the neediness in her voice, but the thought of being alone negated any embarrassment over a possible public breakdown. Appearing needy was the least of her worries. “Just coffee. That’s all.”

He advanced, unhurried and deliberate. “Here’s the problem. I don’t want any coffee. What I want is standing right here. And if I stay, I’m not leaving until I’ve had her.” He reached out and tucked a curl behind her ear.

She swallowed, because holy crap, instead of

clutching her blanket closer, her fingers slackened their grip.

He smudged his thumb over her bottom lip. "So tell me to go or tell me to stay. But do it now."

The corners of the blanket slipped through her fingers allowing it to slide to her feet.

"Decide." His other hand came to rest on her chest. "I want to feel you say it."

Oh, my.

Her hands lingered over his biceps, light as feather down, before they settled across his skin. So warm. Her fingers splayed across his skin and contracted.

He leaned in and touched the skin next to her ear with his lips.

"Say it," he whispered.

Her nails bit into his arms and the muscles under them bunched into rock hard knots.

"Stay." She murmured it to his chest.

He moved his hands to her neck, his thumbs tracing the line of her jaw. He tilted her face up and waited until his eyes were the only thing she saw.

"Mean it."

"Stay."

High grade his-and-her pheromones fogged up the air. She dragged them deep into her lungs, let them seduce her while her fingers danced over his skin. She needed to feel him inside her, deep, deep inside. Where action transcended thought, putting her past caring why she shouldn't. Past caring that she did.

The kitchen shrank, and the air thickened. Every skin cell puckered. A smile tipped the corners of her lips when his chest heaved. Power spiked through her system, forcing her hands up until they were filled with soft bunches of hair.

He brought his hands down, skimmed them over her ultrasensitive breasts, downward, around to her backside. Strong arms lifted her up and against him. Her bare legs wrapped around him and locked. Worn denim scraped against her raw skin. Poised on the brink she stole a second to anticipate. To wonder. To dip and retreat. To decide.

Her lips met his. A hundred thoughts pulsed through her from anxiety, to pleasure, to relief. Old memories, new ones, and the promise of more. Much, much more.

She opened wider, took more of him into her mouth. His flavor, dark, heady, and full-bodied, saturated her tastebuds and triggered a flurry of action.

Her back hit the wall. Warm rough hands pushed their way under her top. Her shirt came off and pooled into a puddle of cotton on the floor. His mouth rushed over her jaw, down her neck, across her collarbone. Blood rushed to places she'd forgotten existed. She pressed closer. She pushed him back. All in a skirmish to gain ground, to come out the winner in a pleasure sweepstakes. A hand slapped against the wall by her ear. His lips continued their downward progress. Relief rushed through her as his tongue circled and his teeth nipped.

He lifted his head and licked his lips. "Again. Slower. Later." Her back slid down the wall, and his hands broke their bodies apart. Her underwear disappeared in a fevered striptease.

"Wait." Pant. "Condom."

"Shit."

"Bedroom. Nightstand. Top Drawer." Tucked way, way back. Possibly expired. *Please, don't be expired.*

"Thank God." His mouth closed over hers again, hot, wet and eager. He wrapped her legs around his waist again. Fitted her against him while his lips tasted and nipped their way along her collarbone, and his legs ate up the distance to her bedroom.

The bed came up to meet them, and they both bounced. Pillows danced around them. The cool sheets granted a temporary relief from the volcanic heat.

“I can’t—”

“Me, either.” She fumbled in a daze with the nightstand drawer handle while he divested himself of his few articles of clothing at warp speed. If only she could beam up the condom with as much efficiency.

“I got it.” He kissed the corner of her mouth. Kept on going, lower and lower, until she felt the tip of his tongue trace the swell of her breast. She shivered at the loss when he stopped and reached over to help dig the elusive condoms out of the very back of the drawer. Package in hand, he ripped it open and slid it on.

She ran her hands over his breadth of shoulder, the skin of his back, the shape and contour of his arms. So warm. So solid. So everything she’d always wanted. His lips found every aching spot. Long fingers skimmed and explored her fluttering stomach, the length of her leg, as he lifted and positioned. Her hands moved up his neck to clench in his ink black hair. She loved his hair. The familiar texture, short now, the scent of it.

He thrust inside her and held fast, waiting before pushing deeper, faster. Her body tightened around him. The universe shrank down to the space between her legs. She dug her heels into his back and tightened her hold on his hair. His body started to buck, and the friction she craved did its work.

Her orgasm tore a hole in the fabric of the universe. The moon rocked, and her heart stopped. Her muscles quivered under the lingering aftershocks. Strands of her hair puffed out into the air as Chase tried to catch his breath.

The silence descended. And it was deafening. Because she was naked. With Chase still inside her. Naked. With Chase. Oh, man. What had she done? Because this was new. *This* had never happened before. Teenage sex had happened before, this was different. This had been earth shattering. At least for her.

"Stop thinking." He laid his forehead against hers. "Okay? Just don't think for the next five minutes."

Sound philosophy, might have worked, if she were a *guy*. And dressed. She closed her eyes as he eased out of her.

"I'll be right back." The bed dipped. She held her breath until she heard the click of the bathroom door.

She plowed her hands through her hair. She'd never thought of sex as something she couldn't live without. Now what was she going to do?

Like she didn't have enough problems.

At the sound of returning feet, she gathered up the sheet, clutched it to her pounding heart. He came through the doorway. Sat down at the edge of the bed. She offered up a prayer of thanks to the crescent moon because it meant neither of them could see a thing.

"Do you want me to leave?" Calloused fingertips caressed her cheek. She turned her face toward them.

"Do you want to leave?" Her vocal cords stuttered over the words.

"Let me rephrase my rhetorical question." When his lips brushed hers, the taste of them, the shape of them, the warmth of them, promised everything she'd convinced herself she didn't need.

Chapter Eight

The first signs of daylight filtered through the clouds gathering off the horizon as Chase's muscles screamed in protest. He pushed them harder, registered the strain. Relished it.

He was a runner. How fucking ironic was that statement? As his arms and legs pumped more speed from a body exhausted to the point of collapse, he refused to stop. Not until the warm, fuzzy images retracted their claws. Not until he sweated the neediness out of his pores. Not until he figured out his next move. Not until he wrapped his mind around a few facts. One in particular.

This was about sex, his past, and a whole bunch of other shit. *Not need.* He wasn't giving up the sex. He wasn't noble or a martyr or an idiot. He was going to take what he could get while he could get it, and make the memory of it last a lifetime. Needing someone more than your next breath cooked up all kinds of crazy.

He needed some freaking perspective back. He needed to be able to keep it bolted to his front and center, even when he was thinking with his dick. Especially when he was thinking with his dick. He couldn't do happily ever after. Shouldn't want to. So he pushed harder and ran until he got it back.

He hit the shower, let the heat and steam ease his muscles, calm his brain. He picked up the soap and washed away Lily's fingerprints. They coated his skin, mapping a trail to every erogenous zone he possessed. Drained, he braced his hands against the shower wall, hung his head, and let the water rain down until it was Arctic cold. Suitably punished, he dried off, dressed, and reached for his personal files. The notes he'd archived on Raphael Tessier and the Prairie Brotherhood.

He brewed coffee, smeared a stale piece of bread with peanut butter, and settled down to pour over the same old information. Add the new stuff to a growing mountain of shit and misery. The process anchored him to the present, to what mattered, and allowed him to focus. He was starting over again from a different direction but one he knew suited his purpose.

With his control questionable at best, but unable to stop himself, he made his way over to Lily's on the guise of inspecting her backyard again, this time in the daylight. She didn't answer the front door, so he made his way around to the back. He walked around the corner and stopped. He should have known. It wasn't smart to leave the woman alone for two minutes, let alone eight hours. Why wasn't she dead tired? Collapsed in a heap? Wasted, like him.

They were searching the yard. The two of them. Looking fresh as daisies, chatting as they went. Something about babies and adorable and family. His heart stuttered at the mention of babies. An unwanted picture of Lily pregnant and laughing up at him ghosted over the everyday scene. He blew it off as he cleared his throat.

Lily tripped over a plant in her haste to turn around. Kate straightened with a gracefulness more in line with a runway than a row of potatoes. They both eyed him with varying degrees of "Oh, it's you." Lily flushed and broke eye contact, hands going to her hair and pushing it back. Kate put her hands on her hips and raised a groomed brow.

"Doing a little gardening?" he asked as he settled in against the deck wall.

Their silent communication spoke volumes, and he sighed. Cohorts since kindergarten, they'd instigated their fair share of trouble. He'd been the recipient of their attentions often enough in the past. Of course, retaliation had its advantages.

Kate picked her way through the rows of vegetables. No mean feat in three-inch heels and a pencil thin skirt. Lily dragged after her, reluctant and uncertain, in a dress the color of cotton candy with giant pink flowers, her feet in rubber boots.

"Nice gardening duds." He crossed his arms.

"Sunday brunch." Kate smoothed a hand over her skirt. "It's a tradition. Just us girls. Girl talk. You know how it goes."

He did and the conversational possibilities had his privates shriveling faster than a dip in winter lake water. Confirmation came by way of the death glare Lily shot at Kate. No need to ask if they'd talked about him.

"Is that what you were doing in the garden? Catching up on girl talk?"

Kate swiped a dainty arm across her forehead, then put a hand on Lily's arm. "I could use a glass of water. Do you mind? Lots of ice. About five minutes worth."

Lily rolled her eyes. "Sure. Chase?"

"Nothing. For now." Water wasn't what he needed, and he wanted her to know it. She blinked and a delightful pink crept under her freckles. It matched her dress. She tensed in warning. Kate mumbled something and pushed Lily toward the deck.

"Behave." Lily pointed a finger at each of them. "I'll be right back."

Kate set a manicured hand against her chest and met his stare head on. "No rush."

He waited until Lily was in the house before he pushed off from the deck. "Long time no see, Kate."

"Chase." She gave him a once-over glance. "So, the bad boy has returned, and as one of the good guys."

He leaned in to kiss her offered cheek. "In a manner of speaking."

"Color me amazed." She brushed a fleck off her skirt. "And just when things are heating up. Your timing is impeccable."

"That must have been quite the brunch."

"Don't blame Lily. I forced things out of her." She offered a faint smile.

"Is this the part where you ask me what my intentions are?" He returned the once-over glance. Spectacular from head to toe and born for high heels.

She ignored him. "I'd rather know how much trouble Lily's landed in."

"Nothing is going to happen to Lily."

"And you're basing that assumption on what?" She cocked a hip.

"On the fact that it will happen over my dead body."

Her eyes stayed cool. "As reassuring as that statement is, I'd feel better knowing you have an actual plan."

He ground his teeth together. "You're going to have to trust me."

Musical laughter filled the air. "Be thankful we have a history, and know if I didn't think I could trust you, believe me, we'd be having a very different conversation right now."

Because they did have a history, and because Kate loved Lily, he attempted an explanation. "Look. I can't go into details."

Kate rolled her eyes and started to interrupt. Chase held up a hand. "Hear me out. I will do whatever it takes to protect her. Starting with keeping a close eye on things."

Her lips twitched. "So it would seem."

"You got a problem with that?"

"I don't know yet. You and Lily…that's between the two of you."

He opened his mouth. She patted him on the cheek and said, "I'll say I'm concerned and leave it at that."

"Duly noted." She wasn't the only one concerned. He was downright freaked out enough for everyone.

"You know she had plans to buy the house you're renting?"

He blinked back surprise. "You've got to be kidding me. What does she want with it? It's a dump." And he should know, he'd paid for university by working construction.

She shrugged. "Thought you should know."

Great, one more way he'd screwed up her life and her plans.

"Do me a favor? Tell Lily I had to go." She paused on her way past him, speared him with a look. "I hope you know what you're doing."

He got she wasn't talking about his job.

Just like he got that he didn't need to turn around to know Lily was standing there wondering what to say, what to avoid saying.

"So you find anything in the yard?" She didn't answer, but he heard her footsteps coming down the deck steps. He didn't imagine they had, like he didn't think she'd seen anyone back there last night. But he was still prepared to do a thorough search on his own. For his own peace of mind. He ran through the possibilities. Likely, no clear shoe or boot impressions left. Trampled plants? Crushed vegetables? Leftover signs.

He wasn't expecting the hand on his arm. Or the silence. Or for her to point to the deck railing, and he sure as hell didn't expect to see a blue bandana tied to one of the posts. Because it hadn't been there last night when he'd searched. He knew that for a fact. Someone had put it there after he and Lily had gone inside and…

While he'd been scratching an itch, Raphael Tessier had sent an edict.

Tagged.

Lily.

In a flash, his blood iced over and his head become a clanging, bell-ringing tower of noise.

Tagged.

Fucking hell.

He charged up onto the deck, ripped the bandana off the post. Tossed it. He wrapped his hands around the top railing and lowered his pulsing head. A growl tore out of him. It had nothing to do with human and everything to do with wild. His heart rate jacked. His skull heated while fear, aggression, and predatory instinct pumped panic through his arteries and spiked it straight to his heart.

His fingers tightened around the deck railing. Soul sucking terror struck like lightning, frying his brain functions.

A dirty alley.

The blood. The guts. The brain matter. Everywhere.

The last time. Conor.

Too late.

Now Lily.

His grip choked the wood as he tried to anesthetize the crippling impotence and tortured sense of failure. He let wrath and fury take its place. The railing creaked and groaned as he pounded at it in a blind haze. He used his boots against it until the narrow spindles cracked under the force and split. Next, a flowerpot shattered against the deck boards, dirt exploding over their feet. Pretty flowers bounced and careened across the deck.

"Chase."

His name. In the distance. The firmness cut through like nothing else could have.

"Stop it. That's enough."

His hands clenched and unclenched at his sides. The breath ripped in and out of him like gunfire. But he could see straight. His line of vision went from blood red to clear in the snap of her fingers.

The broken deck spindles, the ceramic container shards, and clumps of dirt. The crushed flowers.

The destruction.

Caused by him.

"I'm sorry." He reached out a shaking hand. When she grabbed onto it, he pulled her to him, needing to protect, to reassure. He tucked her against him, felt her arms wrap around him. He stole a deep breath, put a hand on the back of her head. Cradled it against his battered heart.

"I'm so sorry." It tumbled out of him, needing to be said. He wanted to say it again. And again. Just like his old man.

She cut him off. "It's significant somehow? The bandana?"

He squeezed his eyes shut before answering. "It is. But don't worry, I'll take care of it. I'll fix it. I promise."

If it took everything he had, he'd put things back together again. This time, no mercy. Because one truth consumed him: Raphael Tessier was a dead man.

All that was left was one lie. "Don't worry. Everything's going to be okay."

****

He was shutting her out and, she was willing to bet, shutting down, too. He'd been on the phone forever conferring with different resources, including Stan Knight, which puzzled her. Gone was the lover from last night, the tortured man from earlier on her deck, here was the police officer, distant, detached and all business.

It was freaking her out.

When he hit *end* she plucked the phone out of his hand and tucked it out of his reach. She ran a hand over her shaky heart. "Talk to me. Please. Avoiding my questions is making it worse, not better."

Her shoulders slumped as he walked across the room to the coffee pot. He poured another cup of coffee with the same deliberation a surgeon wielded a scalpel. He sure as heck didn't need the caffeine. He was keyed up enough, his muscles all but twitching under the casual attitude.

"Coffee?" He lifted the coffee-pot in her direction.

"Can you put some answers in it?"

He abandoned his cup, walked over, and squatted next to her chair. She stared down into eyes he tried to keep cool but burned anyway. Had she really thought him distant? Detached? As scared as she was, she ran a hand over his cheek to reassure him.

"Tell me."

"It's called tagging. Tagged as in target. In their sick minds, it's fair warning." He pulled her hand from his cheek, laid it palm up against one of his, and traced over the lines, her fingers, the tips. He shifted his attention to her face, but not her eyes. Tucked a curl behind her ear. Traced a fingertip along the side of her cheek.

"Target?" Okay, it might be stretching her natural sense of optimism a little far to find something non-terrifying in that one. It didn't sound good. Not any way you looked at it. She swallowed and forced out her next question. "A target how?"

He kissed the center of her palm. Sweet gesture or more stalling? He smoothed a finger over the spot.

"As in human target. Intimidation. It's a warning they'll do whatever it takes to get what they want."

Her fingers folded over his, squeezed and held on tight. "But I don't have what they want. I don't even know what it is."

"All the more reason to trust me."

She hesitated. "I do. But I still can't help them."

"They don't care. I know what I'm talking about here. Trust me."

"I do. I trust you with my life." Her heart was another matter.

"Good. That's good." The grimness receded a bit. "Then you'll listen when I say you need to leave. At least for a while, until we get this situation straightened out."

She slipped her hand free of his. "What? No. I'm not leaving. That's like giving into them. Giving them what they want."

"No, it's not. It's about staying safe." The grimness was back. His hands went to the arms of her chair, closing her in. She refused to let him know his coercion tactics were working. But her fear was a wet blanket she couldn't throw off.

She braced her back against her chair. "How is my leaving going to help Jason?"

He stretched to his full height. "I promise you. We'll look after Jason, even if I have to babysit him twenty-four seven myself."

Her head moved side-to-side. "No. I haven't done anything wrong. I'm not running away from this, or from them. You need to understand and accept it. I'm not going to make it easier for them. I'm not leaving Jason, I'm not leaving my job, or my friends, or my life." *Or you.*

"But you'll make it hard for us. For me. What if I can't save you both?" His hands sifted through his hair before landing on his hips.

"It's not your job to save me. To protect me—yes,

within the limits of what your job demands. But I make my own decisions. And I'm not leaving. You should be working on getting Jason out of here instead."

Pushing past him, she beat a path to the living room and paused in front of her big picture window. The scene was so normal. So every day of her life. Today showed the first signs of autumn, with its hints of red and gold, faded grass, late blooming flowers. Nothing telegraphed terrorists, vicious gangs, or violence. No neon sign flashing danger. No disclaimers. Just a square of blue and white cotton, a gang bandana, tied to a piece of wood railing in her backyard.

She watched her neighbor across the street unlock her toddler from his car seat, then unload her groceries from her SUV. They were renovating, turning it into their dream home, the neighbor had confided. So happy. So normal. So lucky.

Chase came up behind her. "Would it make any difference if I said we were working on it? If I said the reason they're coming after you is because they're finding it next to impossible to get to Jason?"

She fixated on the scene unfolding across the street. The little boy ran up and wrapped his arms around his mother's legs. His mom bent down and kissed his hair. "No, it doesn't."

"Lily, this...situation with us, it's a distraction I don't need right now. A couple of days would give me some time to get things under control."

Wow, reality check. She was a *distraction*. One he wanted gone. "After last night? You still want me to leave?"

"Yes." His tone left no room for misunderstandings.

She shut her eyes tight. She thought about Jason, alone and frightened, with nowhere to turn. At least her way left Raphael Tessier with two targets and twice the headache. She cleared her throat and squared her shoulders. "Whatever you're planning, you're going to need to do it with me in town. I'm not going anywhere."

His ringing cell phone saved her from further argument. He marched back into the kitchen to answer. All she heard was "Stan, what's up?" and a sense of foreboding put her heart in a vise-grip and squeezed. She closed her eyes and fought against the panic.

She didn't want to know.

To keep her brain from exploding, she counted back from one thousand and mumbled her way to four hundred and seventy-three before he reappeared. He entered the room the way he'd left, in a hurry.

"I have to leave."

She needed to get used to hearing those words. "Of course. It's okay. I'll be fine."

"I'll be back." He must have sensed her anxiety, because he frowned. "Soon. I promise."

She lifted her hand and shooed him off. "Go. Do what you have to do. I'll be here."

He crossed the room and kissed the top of her head. "Think about what I said earlier. Just a couple of days. That's all I'm asking."

"Right. Get rid of the distraction. I know, I get it."

"That's not what I meant." But he lied, and they both knew it.

"No, it's okay. It's good to know where I stand."

"Hey. Look at me." He tilted her chin up. "You're not just a distraction. Okay? You never were. It's always been more than that."

But how much more? How much more did she want? How much was healthy? Her head weighed a ton. She let it drop to his chest. He smelled the same. Edgy, impatient—were those scents? Her cheek nuzzled the soft cotton of his shirt as she locked her arms around his waist. Did she trust him? Did she trust herself?

He pulled back, ran a hand over her hair, and lifted her chin so they were eye to eye. "I'll be back as soon as I can."

A quick nod. He headed for the door.

****

Chase slid into the passenger seat of Stan Knight's spotless late model sedan, which was parked under the shade of an ancient poplar tree one street over from where his fellow officers were searching and securing the McCarran residence. His day wasn't getting any better, not by a long shot. A home invasion in broad daylight. Raphael Tessier was getting desperate. Good in some ways. So very bad in others.

Chase watched out the window. "You get a good look at them?"

"Three of them. Your man, Tessier, and two others. All of them sporting the right colors. No visible weapons." Stan picked up his bottle of diet soda and gulped some back. "I called in an anonymous tip."

"Jason?"

"No one was home. He and his old man are at the aunt's house. But I had a bad feeling so I doubled back, kept an eye out for a while. Sure enough, not five minutes later they showed up."

Sooner or later they'd get to Jason. He was running out of lives faster than a cat in a pen of salivating wild dogs. For now, he'd count his blessings and be thankful for the fact Jason hadn't been in residence. He'd take the break, and be grateful for it. But that didn't mean desperation wasn't clawing his insides to shreds.

"They see you?"

The older man snorted his disapproval. "Hell,

no. And I'm insulted you should ask."

Chase smirked. "They leave with anything?"

"Impossible to tell, but nothing visible. Tessier didn't look very happy, and they left in a hurry."

"How long were they in there?" The last thing he wanted was a happy Tessier. The thought made his skin crawl.

"Not long. Two minutes, max. Not long enough to do a thorough search of the place."

Which meant they were looking for someone instead of something. "You see which way they went?"

"Please, who do think you're talking to, boy? Not only saw but followed. Only for a bit, though, before I had to let him go.

Chase clapped his mentor on the shoulder. "Happens to the best of us. You feel up for a drive? See if we can pick up the trail?"

Stan put the car into drive, slipped back out onto the street and headed west.

****

Not knowing was killing her. Before he'd left, she hadn't wanted to know. Now here she sat, drumming her fingertips on the arm of her chair, regretting the weakness. She stretched out her legs to inspect her pedicure and sighed over a chipped nail. Had there really been a time when something so trivial registered on her radar?

Maybe she should...

No, not a good idea. Nowhere would that be considered a good idea. But...

She jumped when the phone rang. Keeping her fingers crossed, she grabbed for the receiver. "Hello."

"You got no idea the kind of trouble's gonna rain down on you."

"What?" The edges of her vision blurred as she gripped the receiver. "Who is this?"

"I'm insulted." His voice, gravel pit low, scraped

over her raw nerves.

"What do you want?" she whispered. The phone quaked in her hand. She gripped her wrist with her other hand to steady it. *Think. Think. Think.*

"Tag. You're it." He enunciated each word.

She pictured him smiling and smug as he chose his words, handpicked the ones to terrify her. She pushed out of her chair, revolted. "I'm not playing your sick games."

"I want what the kid has. You're going to get it for me. It's do or die time, little teacher."

"And if I can't get it?" Because really, what if she couldn't?

"Then you both die." So matter of fact.

"You touch one hair on his head—"

He laughed. "And you'll do what?"

"I mean it. You leave him be." Her feet rooted to the floor while her brain spun in circles.

"Then it's all on you. Get me what I want. And keep your mouth shut."

She nodded.

"Are we clear?" he repeated.

She nodded once more before she remembered to answer out loud. "Yes."

"Pretty dress. Pink looks good on you."

The line went dead. She parachuted past shaky and nauseous to undone in a puff of panic. She glanced down at the huge pink flowers scattered over her pink dress. She clamped a hand over her mouth as she swung to the right. Pressed her body against a solid wall, away from her picture window. Out of the line of sight.

The shaking derailed her attempt to set the phone down. It hit the floor a second before her knees did the same. Tears threatened. She shut them down. No time for hysterics. She needed a plan.

So she put things to right as much as she could,

changed her clothes, redid her makeup, and opened a bottle of wine. The first glass was medicinal, the second numbing, the third unnecessary and frankly not as helpful as she expected. To clear her head and give her hands a job, she decided to go ahead and make supper. If Chase showed up, eating would buy her some time. Distract him, the way to a man's heart and all that. She'd thought long and hard about her next move. Raphael Tessier was intent on terrifying her into doing what he ordered. But bottom line, Chase would sense something was up. She was a bad liar and a worse actor.

She had to tell him.

Didn't she?

Of course, she did. She ripped up lettuce and stuffed the shredded bits into a large bowl. He was the professional. She needed his help, as long as his help didn't include packing her suitcase and shipping her off to the other side of the world, whether she wanted to go or not. Her chef's knife hit the cutting board, severing peppers from their insides.

Buy time to think. To choose her words. To spin things her way.

Falling to pieces served no reasonable purpose. Her new mantra: Stay calm at all costs. She guillotined a cucumber. The garden fresh tomato went next. She'd taken pretty darn good care of herself the last few years, since her parents' retirement to the coast. In the years before their move, too. They'd raised her to be independent. To make good choices. To trust her instincts.

Her instincts said to stay right here in Aspen Lake. She grabbed some strawberries from her fridge and started chopping. Tell Chase about the phone call, but maybe leave out the part about the dress. The whole "do it or die" threat. The strawberry bits landed in the salad bowl. She refilled her wine glass.

That way she wasn't lying per se, simply choosing to play some cards closer to her chest. She retrieved some leftover grilled chicken from the fridge and before long, it lay sliced and diced. The green onions sacrificed themselves to the cause, and the walnuts dissolved to dust under her knife. Cooking always soothed her.

By the time her front doorbell rang, her glass was empty. She hung it upside down and shook it. The doorbell rang again. She frowned, then remembered. She raced to the door and peeked through the eye hole before opening the door.

He was back.

"Thank heavens, you're safe." Her hands went every direction, checking and cataloguing; making sure he was okay, in one piece, whole.

His hands closed over her shoulders, and he pushed her back a step. "Hey, are you okay?"

He was getting spooky. "I'm fine. I'm cooking."

He dropped his arms and stepped into the hallway. "In the dark? Why are all the blinds closed?"

"I closed them. Keeps it cooler." She stumbled back a step and covered it up with a laugh. "I thought you'd be back sooner. I was worried. I'm allowed to be worried, aren't I? After all, I now know you have a mole on the inside of your left thigh. I didn't know that before, can you believe it?"

"Are you drunk?" His head blurred to the right.

She tsked. "No."

He moved past her into the kitchen and looked around. "So nothing happened while I was gone?"

"Nothing." She crossed her chest with two fingers. "You are a very suspicious person, did you know that? I don't remember you being this suspicious. I made salad."

"Really. Was that before or after you finished

this? He dangled the empty bottle of wine from his fingers.

"I happen to be a very good cook. And I am not drunk."

"Right." He set the bottle back down and put his hands on her cheeks. "But you'd tell me if something happened?"

"Absolutely." At some point in time or another, she absolutely would.

He'd been watching her. Watching them.

Watching as her life sped out of control. She shivered. "Right now, I'd rather do this." She kissed him smack on the lips.

"Lily, I don't think this is a good—"

She fumbled her way to his belt buckle and oblivion. She didn't get as far as she hoped. He picked her up and carried her to bed. He tucked the covers in around her and settled in beside her.

"Get some sleep."

"I don't want to sleep." But she did. Just like this. Forever. Her eyes drooped as her body sagged in relief. Just like this forever.

Chapter Nine

Lily popped two more ibuprofen before leaving her classroom because her hair still hurt. She was toasted, roasted, and fried, with no viable plan to avoid deportation to Safe According to Chase Nowhereville. Raphael Tessier's demands haunted her. Jason needed her. She was falling in love with her costar from their little drama of horrors, and he wasn't falling in love back.

Again.

Was there a pill for that?

After classes were through for the day, she'd met with a couple of teachers to collaborate on a joint project. Meeting over, they all made their way to their cars together. In light of the attacks on Jason, there was now supervision of the grounds by the staff until all students were off the property. Jason's aunt had agreed to take him to school and pick him up afterward until the danger had passed. The teachers had agreed to leave in pairs.

The reassuring click of her car lock echoed, and she laughed at her co-worker's lame joke as he paused by her car. She opened her car door. Out of the corner of her eye, she caught a glimpse of a white piece of folded paper laying on the driver's seat. An ordinary white sheet of paper, but nothing she had left there earlier in the day. A dull buzz filled her head as she finished with her goodbyes. In a daze, she watched the other teacher approach his truck before scanning the lot. She squinted at hedges rimming the property before canvassing the almost empty lot. Nothing.

Using the edges of her fingernails, she lifted the note as she slid into the driver's seat. She shut and locked the doors, then careful to touch only the barest edge, unfolded the note.

A small thump on her car door window upped the terror ante. The note slipped from her fingers and dropped to the floor as her heart sky-dived into action. Her eyes slid left, expecting to see a tattooed face. Instead, she spied her co-worker getting ready to tap on the window again. She closed her eyes as her shoulders slumped, and her brain plotted a course back from scared sick. One hand went to her heart, the other went to the window button.

"Sorry didn't mean to startle you. Forgot to give you this on the way out. Thought you might want it." A file appeared in the open window as he frowned. "Sorry again. Sure you're okay?"

She nodded. "Yeah, I'm fine. A little jumpy, you know? See you tomorrow." She smiled and set the file on the passenger seat. "Thanks."

She tracked his progress to his truck in her rearview window before bending down to retrieve the piece of paper from under her shoe. Her uneasy fingers unfolded the edges. She swallowed as the large black, sloppy message became visible.

Bitch. I can get to you any time. Anywhere. You have 24 hours.

Her fingers managed a methodical refolding before the shudders overtook her. Her hand convulsed around the edges of the paper until it collapsed and disappeared inside her fist. The ball of paper dropped to her lap. She dropped her aching head to the steering wheel. Blindly, she twisted the key, letting the pulse of the engine soothe her tangled nerves. She would figure it out. She would.

She had to.

****

Chase swore he heard his back teeth crack and figured in another five minutes, he'd be spitting chunks of enamel. Jason's father was exhausting his limited supply of patience. It had been a long shot to think a man like Jake McCarran would give a crap about someone or something other than his pride or his next drink.

Chase leaned back in his chair and signaled Mike to take over the interview. He studied Jason, who'd been glaring at the same spot on the table since he'd dragged his butt into the room and dropped into the chair ten minutes ago.

Time was running out. They needed to find his brother before Raphael Tessier and the Prairie Brotherhood did. Intel gathered from shared police databases and former contacts confirmed what his gut told him every five minutes. If they didn't, Kevin McCarran was as good as dead.

"I keep telling you I don't know where he is! Haven't seen or heard from him in over a year." The old man's fists connected with the tabletop. "I ain't telling you again."

"Mr. McCarran, please try and understand. We're only concerned for his safety. The Prairie Brotherhood are ruthless people and if they believe Kevin cheated them or wronged—"

"That's a lie. My son did no such thing." Spittle flew out of his nasty mouth with its foul breath and yellowed teeth.

Chase had to hand it to Mike. The guy kept his cool. His own methods ran a little more to the right and went a little less by the book. But even Mr. Cool was starting to look like he wanted to beat something bloody.

Mike tried again. "We're not saying he did. We're trying to figure out motive. Paramount to us is keeping your sons safe." Mike shifted in Jason's direction. "Jason, the men who attacked you? Did they mention your brother?"

Jake McCarran gave his son a shove. "Answer the man. Tell him you don't know nothing about this."

Chase straightened. A tide of bile started to rise, and he pushed it back, like he did every damn time he saw a kid take a shove, or a punch, or a slap. And it royally pissed him off that he couldn't stop his toes from twitching inside his regulation black boots like he was still ten years old and helpless.

He leaned in and made sure the old man knew eye contact wasn't optional. "Mr. McCarran. Shove your son one more time, and I'm going to get angry."

"You threatening me, boy?" He snorted air out through his nose, then swiped at it with his sleeve.

Mike snapped a file shut. "Come on, Mr. McCarran, let me get you a coffee. Jason's fine to stay here."

"No damn way. I know my rights. His too. You just finished spouting off about how neither of them is in trouble."

"Not in any legal trouble, no. But you need to heed the fact their safety is in question."

"I look after my own." His chest puffed out like a stringy little bantam rooster's. "Now get up. We're leaving." He lifted his hand, but let it fall after a quick peek at Chase.

Chase caught Mike's eye and tilted his head in Jason's direction.

Mike stood, put his hands on his hips. "Mr. McCarran, there's a paper I need you to sign."

"I'm not signing nothing." He crossed his arms and shifted his ass as if super gluing it to the chair.

Mike shrugged. "It's a formality only. Also, there's not likely going to be a reward for information, and it won't amount to much if there is, but they like to keep track of addresses, phone numbers, etc."

"Money?"

"Yeah, sometimes Crime Stoppers offers a reward for information."

"Typical." The old man slapped his hands onto the table and pushed off the chair. He pointed a shaking finger at Mike. "I'll sign the damn thing, and you can check out the reward thing for me, but then we're leaving."

"Come on then, the paper's on my desk."

Chase used the opportunity to stall Jason's exit while Jake McCarran beat a path after Mike. "Okay, we've got one minute here, max. I can help you, but I need you to be honest with me and tell me what's going on with your brother."

Silence.

"Look, I know he's in trouble. So are you. But the Prairie Brotherhood is not going anywhere. You can't keep avoiding them. You've been lucky so far, but that luck's going to run out. You need my help."

"I can't tell you. I can't." Jason shoved his hands into his pants pockets and focused on the scarred floor. "They'll hurt Kevin."

"Not if we find him first." Chase resisted the urge to shake him. Instead, he glanced over his shoulder, then pulled out a pen and paper and scribbled down his number. "Take my number. Call anytime, day or night. I can help you. You can trust me. I can help Kevin, too. Just give me a chance to prove it."

Jason's thin body jerked when his dad yelled his name. He hesitated, stole a glance in his father's direction, reached out and accepted the paper. He stuffed it into the front pocket of his jeans and nodded. One slight downward motion of his head, but it was all Chase needed to see.

He breathed a sigh of relief. Finally—a break.

His best friend, a damn good cop, was dead because of Raphael Tessier and the Prairie Brotherhood. For the first time, the noose of justice was tightening around Raphael Tessier's throat. The Enforcer was scrambling. Now all Chase needed to do was keep everyone safe while he jerked on the rope.

****

Lily answered her door with her twenty-four hour deadline hanging over her head. It might as well be twenty-four days. She had no plan, no idea what she was supposed to get from Jason. She wasn't a magician; she couldn't conjure up whatever it was Tessier was desperate to get his hands on. She was an educator. She'd sworn to use her powers for good, not evil.

What was she supposed to tell Chase that wouldn't get him killed? Or her deported? With one hand braced over her heart, she opened the door. Her body reacted at the sight of him. He'd changed from his uniform into street clothes and was lounging against the railing, holding an empty coffee mug.

She raised an eyebrow at the sight of the cup.

"I was hoping I could borrow a little sugar." He jiggled the cup in his hand.

"Really." She tilted her head and looked him over.

"Yes, Ma'am."

"Sorry, Officer, I'm all out of sugar." Also low on common sense and scraping the bottom of the barrel on fortitude, but who was keeping track? Not her hormones. What she had in abundance was a declining mental state whose bad decision-making skills were leading her toward a permanent body rocking state.

He stepped forward, placed a finger under her chin and gently coaxed her face upward. "That's okay, we'll have our morning coffee without sugar."

"Do you actually think that corny line's going to work on me?" But she was smiling, a full body smile. Her toes curled, her fingers twitched, her skin sang, and her treacherous heart beat a little faster.

"Yeah. I do." He grinned, and since those grins were as rare as wild orchids, it almost made her forget.

Almost.

But not quite.

Twenty-four hours. She snuck a peek at her watch—make that twenty hours, forty-seven minutes, and thirteen seconds. She needed to bring him up to speed. Confide in him. Trust him.

Heavy lidded, he leaned in, and an image flashed into place, all fuzzy around the edges, of them in bed drinking coffee, sharing the paper and a bagel. Those fantasy photographs were getting harder and harder to dismiss or push back. The mental white picket boards were going up faster than he could tear them down.

He chuckled and reached for her hand. In an effort to keep things playful, she dodged him. The sexy smile she offered up lured him to follow her into the brightly lit kitchen. The sight of the shuttered patio doors stopped her short. She wished she could fling them open, escape onto her deck with its open air and collection of stars and space. The clink of his cup landing on her counter sounded in the background. His footsteps signaled his approach. She closed her eyes and waited. He came up behind her, wrapped his arms around her. So solid. So warm. So appealing.

He reached out a hand to open the doors, and she grabbed hold of his hand to stop him. "No. Leave them closed."

"Hey." He pulled her around to face him and frowned. "What's going on? Is something wrong?"

Be wise. Be strong. Trust him.

She bit her bottom lip before asking, "Do you remember when we were kids?"

The shield went up, or the curtain came down, whatever explanation best fitted the thing that happened to his face, his demeanor, his eyes, when the past came up. They shifted from crystal blue and inviting to icy and guarded in less than a nanosecond. It told her everything she wanted to know. He wasn't going to open up to her. Ever.

She wanted him back. And he wasn't coming.

"I remember *you*." His arms tightened.

Her heart sighed, and the scent of him cast a spell. A trace of soap, a whiff of man, and a fragrance so familiar it made her think of bush parties, bonfires, cheap wine, and the back seat of an '86 Firebird.

She remembered every little detail.

"What's this about, Lilypad?"

That he remembered that awful nickname he'd labeled her with when they were kids was a visceral punch to the gut.

She wrinkled her nose. "I hated that name."

"I know. I'd have been disappointed if you hadn't."

"Why 'Lilypad'?"

"I don't know. I thought of it one day when a bunch of us were catching frogs."

"You're such a sweet talker."

He hadn't moved an inch, yet he seemed closer. "You don't want a sweet talker. Remember?" He ran a finger down the side of her cheek. "You want someone who's going to let you know exactly what he plans to do to you. And believe me, there won't be anything sweet about it."

In the second needed to catch her breath, she changed her mantra to: Live in the moment. Forget Tessier and his bag of terrors. Forget everything. For the next hour. One more hour.

"Promises, promises." She backed up slowly, leading him in the right direction until her butt hit the table. He stalked her step for step, eyes focused. A lone wolf, hungry and closing in on his prey. She parried with a siren's smile.

"You have no idea." His lips hit the soft spot behind her ear as he lifted her up and set her down on the table, the motion and disruption of air displacing the few odds and ends littering the tabletop. "The things I want to do to you in the dark. I've had ten years to plan."

One second short of just-in-time she remembered the note. Out of the corner of her eye she saw the scrap of crumpled paper bounce. Her hand shot out to catch it, but the whoosh of air sent it over the edge and sailing to the floor.

"Leave it. This is more important." Strong hands palmed her cheeks, soft lips tasted hers. Her eyelids drifted shut and her focus shifted from the threatening note to his warmth. To his tongue in her mouth, dancing with hers. She was lost in a place she'd never need a map to find. Her fingers brushed against the skin of his arms and traveled up until they were entwined in his hair.

Yes. Forget the note. The note terrified her. She needed this. This crash and burn to get her through the next few hours.

He pulled back. "Bed."

Definitely. Bed. "Yes."

She backed up a finger length, and her lips curved. A surge of power shot through her system. The columns of his neck were taut, his heavy eyelids concealed nothing. It was an incredible turn on, that perfect combination of ferocious and desperate. It cranked her ebbing self-confidence up a notch.

She pushed him back and slipped down from the table. Hallway, bedroom, bed. She headed out of the room, a quick glance over her shoulder hinting at every sinful thought parading past her psyche.

He growled and moved forward, the crumpled paper note disappearing under his booted foot. The crunch of paper caused her smile to slip a notch. She hesitated for a half second, willed him forward over the damning little piece of paper before turning away and shutting her eyes. Her prayer for interference fraught with assurances of wiser behavior in the future. She faced back around to assess the damage.

Two little lines appeared between his brows as he stopped. He stepped to the side, bent and grabbed up the note. He grinned at her as he straightened and started to toss it back onto the table. A little mini whoosh of breath escaped before she could stop it. She forced her lips to curve, trying to get her smile back.

Then something caught his eye. Some word—likely "Bitch."

His grin disappeared. She gave up any pretense at maintaining one. She closed her eyes as those gorgeous colorful threads of lust slowly unraveled.

The sound of paper crumpling forced her eyes open.

"How long have you had this?"

"Not long." She swallowed. "I found it this afternoon."

"Where?"

"Inside my car. After school." Options. She wanted options. Anything but the truth.

"How many people have seen it, touched it."

"Just me. And you."

"Perfect. It's next to useless." He tossed it on the table. "Care to explain what this is about? And when you were going to tell me about it? Save us both some time and start with the truth. I don't want another lie."

"I didn't lie. I never said there wasn't a note."

But it was semantics, and they both knew it.

"Twenty-four hours for what?" Playful went out the patio doors. Lust hit the floor and scattered to the far corners of the room. Disappointment and hurt cruised over his features before he turned his face away.

She wrapped her arms around her middle and managed another swallow past a throat as dry as dust. She was so stupid, and stubborn, and scared. She wasn't thinking straight.

"Lily?"

"To find out whatever Jason knows." She couldn't do this by herself. She didn't know how. Her stubbornness was going to get someone she loved killed.

"And that's the whole truth?"

"Mostly."

"What else?" His hands locked onto his hips.

"He said—" She looked past him to stare at the wall.

"You talked to him? When?"

Her hand went to her throat and massaged the area over her larynx, willing the words out.

"At some point you're going to have to trust me."

"Same goes." She squared her shoulders and lifted her chin.

He didn't acknowledge her words. He clutched at the back of his head and stared at the ceiling. "Yesterday. While I was gone? What happened?" His arms fell to his sides as his gaze swung back to her.

"Chase—"

"Tell me."

"I didn't mean to lie to you."

"But you did."

She gasped out a small laugh as she went on the offensive. "We're going to make this about honesty? Seriously?"

"If you're referring to a decade ago, and I

assume you are, because it always comes down to that, I did what I had to do. For both of us."

Her eyebrows shot up. "Excuse me?"

"And what if I were to tell you we're already halfway to finding out what Jason knows?"

"That changes everything." Hope bloomed in her chest. She searched his face. When he didn't say anything else, just watched her, she reached out a hand only to be rebuffed. She let it drop. "Is it true?"

"We'll get to that in a minute. Anything else you want to tell me? Now would be a good time."

The dark outside her door shape-shifted and the urge to run overwhelmed her. Her monster wasn't locked in a closet or hiding under her bed. He existed in real time. He was loose and free, determined with no conscience. Her shoulders slumped. "He phoned. Raphael Tessier. Jason has something he wants. He's demanding I retrieve it for him." While she was busy confessing, he'd gotten closer. She reached up a hand and smoothed it over his chest.

He wasn't done. "Finish it."

"He'd been watching me. He knew what I was wearing. He said..." She put her hand over her mouth to hide the quivering, but her eyes filled up, giving her away. "He said to keep my mouth shut."

He uttered a string of oaths.

She concentrated on blinking and swallowed a huge gulp of air. "I wanted to tell you, but…"

"But you didn't."

"No. I didn't." She was so done with lying. She stunk at it anyway.

He stared at her, trying to decipher her intentions, and then he pulled his cell phone out of his pocket and dialed.

"Yeah, it's me. I need authorization for patrol cars to provide surveillance for the night at the residences of Lily Wheeler and Jake McCarran. Call me back. Thanks."

"See, this is exactly what I didn't want to happen."

"They're not just threatening you. Jason is going to take the brunt of this." He picked up the note and stuffed it into the back pocket of his jeans.

She followed him as he marched over to the big picture window in the living room. He pulled aside the curtain, then let it drop back into place. "Tomorrow you're having a security alarm installed."

"Wait a minute. This is still my house."

"It's either a security alarm, or we pull valuable manpower otherwise occupied in hunting down members of the Prairie Brotherhood to babysit you."

"That's not fair. I don't want that and you know it. This is my life—"

"I need to know you're safe. As safe as I can make you. So I can do my damn job." He made his way to a side window, pushed aside the drapes, and looked out, then glanced back at her. Something in her expression must have caused him to detour back to where she stood.

"I need you to do this for me." He stared at her, waited for her to speak then shook his head and rounded the corner.

"Wait a minute. Where are you going?" She followed, scrambling to keep up and collided into him as he yanked open the front door.

"I have to go."

****

Chase stalked to the end of Lily's driveway. No patrol car in sight. It left him with nothing to do but wait. To think. Escaping the exposure of the streetlights, he stepped onto the darker street. Tessier was watching her. He strove for a sense of professional composure as he searched the street. An empty construction disposal bin across the way. Vehicles parked in driveways, on the street. Homes with lights on, others dark. Empty backyards with tall trees, dense shrubbery, and storage sheds. Tessier could be anywhere.

She'd played him. Lying by omission was playing him. The knowledge burned. He rolled his shoulders, trying to ease the tension caused by frustration, and hurt pride. It didn't mean he was giving up. He yanked out his cell phone.

"Hey, it's me. Can you meet me at Mary's in five minutes?" He snapped his phone shut.

Her ability to turn him inside out and upside down six ways from Sunday hadn't waned. Ten years later, she'd added the power to scare him spitless to her arsenal of tricks. Picturing her lying broken and bleeding was enough to send him over the edge.

She didn't trust him. She'd kept the threatening messages from him at the expense of her personal safety. That spoke volumes. He was never going to get that back. It was time to face facts. To change tactics. Car lights swung onto the quiet street. He squinted into the dark.

He waved the oncoming patrol over. He left instructions and headed for his vehicle. Three minutes later, he walked into Mary's and headed for the back booth.

"Thanks for meeting me." Chase slid in behind the table and righted the cup in front of him.

"Are you kidding, I haven't had this much fun in months. I feel ten years younger already." Stan signaled the waitress.

"Ruth okay with all this?"

Stan shrugged. "She understands. So what's up?"

Chase paused as the waitress filled his cup and left. "Tessier's been watching Lily."

"Son of a bitch."

"I know. The thing is, there're only so many places to watch from and I want to find that spot."

"Okay. I'll take a look around. I assume you'll be

reporting all this in an official capacity." It wasn't a question.

"Yeah, but I wanted to give you a head's up. See if you could snoop around a little on your own. Report anything you find. Either to me or Mike." Chase gulped a mouthful of coffee.

"You're hoping he'll use the spot again." Stan settled back against the booth.

"Got it in one. He has to screw up sooner or later, and this just might be the place for it to happen."

"How's Lily holding up?"

"Fine."

"Fine? What kind of answer is that?"

"The only one I've got."

"Isn't it time you admitted you've never gotten over that girl? Do something about it?"

"It's not that simple." Chase pushed his coffee cup away. The last thing he needed was more caffeine.

"The hell it isn't." Stan leaned forward and crossed his lean, ropey arms on the table.

"Look, I burnt that bridge a long time ago."

Stan stabbed a finger in his direction. "No, you look. People can be stupid over a lot of different things: alcohol, money, women. Don't let family be the thing that makes you stupid."

"That's not all there is to it, and you know it." Chase wanted to bang his head against something very hard. He had his reasons and they were good ones.

"This had better not be about your gene pool. That's just going to piss me off. I showed you better than that."

"I can't change who I am."

"No, you can't, and you shouldn't. But I'd be willing to bet Lily knows who you are, warts and all. She's not the kind you screw around with; she's the type you marry."

The old man still had the power to make him squirm. "I'm not marrying anyone."

"Your choice. Just make sure it's for the right reasons." Stan tossed a five dollar bill onto the table. "I'll talk to you tomorrow?"

"Yeah. Tomorrow."

Chase sat back. *The kind you marry.* He didn't know anything about marriage. He knew about statistics. The high rate of divorce among police officers. What happened when a cop was married to his job first and foremost? What happened when the only thing you remembered from your childhood was abuse? He couldn't do it. Not to her.

He hadn't given her up ten years ago to see her terrorized and brutalized now. He would have Raphael Tessier's head on a pike. If he so much as touched one hair on her head, he'd hunt Tessier down and deal with him like a rabid dog.

Chapter Ten

Lily peered through the tiny peephole in her door early the next morning, expecting to see her babysitter of the hour. No such luck. It was that other guy. The one her bones ached over, the one she lost sleep over, the one she wanted despite the attitude, the abrasive personality, and his history. She tugged on the sleeves of her favorite sweater and braced herself for the cool breeze, heavy gray clouds, and the disapproval waiting for her on her stoop.

"Joe said to say thanks for the coffee and the muffin." He handed her an empty coffee cup and plate.

"Well, tell Joe it was the least I could do after he sat out there half the night." She reached for the dishes and tried to get a read on Chase's mood. The disapproval was there, but it was thin and disguising something deeper.

"I arranged for someone to come over here today and install a security alarm." Not a question. No request for affirmation. A statement of fact.

"And good morning to you, too. I've got about half-an-hour before I need to be at work." She offered a cool little smile. "I was about to have coffee. You?"

"I need you to let me do this." He possessed very few tells. But the tic along his jaw line was a dead giveaway every time.

And because it was also in his voice, something

of the lover underneath the tougher-than-titanium cop exterior, she filled two cups, handed him one. She was done with being and feeling stupid. Besides, the alarm system made perfect sense. That didn't mean she had to make it easy on him.

"Why?" She held up a hand. "The real why. No standard operating procedure. Because this isn't the policeman talking, this is the man. So, please, be straight with me."

His jaw flexed, and his body stretched. He started to pace the tiny space. "Because I feel guilty enough as it is and it would rip my guts out if anything happened to you. I know what he's capable of, the lengths he'll go to. The thought of you standing in his way.... You're the one person in the world whose safety means everything to me. So, please, let me do what I can to protect you. To keep you safe. To give you a future."

"All right." She swallowed a giant lump of *sweet mercy*. Knew she was missing a deeper something beyond the heartbreaking implication of *for now* and *after I leave*.

His chest rose with one deep breath and fell. "Good, I'll arrange it."

She nodded again. He approached, one cautious step at a time, and laid a hand along her jaw line, his thumb brushing over her lips, his gaze locked on them.

"I can't tell you—" She watched his eyes close, open, and focus on her. "I need you to trust me. I know that's a lot to ask. But I need to know it's true."

In love with him. So very much in love with him. The man. She'd been "in love" with the boy, so in love with the boy. But had she ever really loved him? Maybe a seventeen-year-old version of it, what she knew about it coming from books, movies. An innocent and pure heart had loved the idea of him. A warrior, even then, strong, loyal, and fierce.

Her eighteen-year-old warrior.

But he wasn't a teenager anymore, and neither was she. Time to start the adult version of the story. To love him in the true sense of the word. Not the fairytale version. Him. Whether he stayed or whether he left.

"I trust you." Because it was true, she did trust him. With her life. She'd done some serious thinking in the dark, done some recalibrating. Thought like the grown up she'd become in the last ten years. It didn't mean she was ready to share how she felt. Not when it was ready to gush out of her crazy style. "I do."

"Thank you." He bent and rested his forehead against hers. "Last night. I'm sorry I left the way I did. It won't happen again. Cross my heart and hope to—"

She placed a finger against his lips. "Don't even say it."

He wrapped warm fingers around hers, his eyes wary. "There's more, and I don't want you to say anything until you've heard me out."

She cringed at what was coming, the whole leaving-is-the-best-option speech. "I'm not leaving while Jason is still here. I'm just not. And this isn't about trusting you. I do trust you. I do. But I just can't do it."

"Will you just listen? It's not what you're thinking, but it's the best option we've got right now. Those twenty-four hours are running out, and there's no telling what Tessier will do next, but it's going to be bad."

"I'm listening."

"We've come up with a plan, and we need your help."

She blinked, waited for the "but." When it didn't make an appearance, she started nodding and couldn't stop. Her tiny beam of hope manifested itself into a big grin. "Yes. For sure. Anything."

He stepped back. "No. None of that. Don't read more into this then there is. It's not like I'm deputizing you. Okay? It isn't anything like the scenario I can tell you're dreaming up. There are strict conditions. Lots of them."

His radio went off, jerking them out of the moment. Lily tried to grasp the meaning of the mess of numbers pouring through his radio, but they meant nothing to her. Chase pressed a button as he exited the room, his face grim and his stride long. The walls and the buzzing in her ears muddled the rest of the alert. She listened for the slam of the door. Instead, Chase stalked back into the kitchen.

"What? What is it?"

Chase put a hand on her arm and that scared her worse than anything.

"Jason's aunt just reported him missing."

"Missing? What kind of missing? On his own missing, or 'taken' missing?"

"As in he's gone."

"Gone where? What do we do now?"

"I have to go."

"You don't think Jason's gone to meet Raphael Tessier do you?" That horrifying thought terrified her most of all.

"I don't know what to think." He placed his hands on her shoulder, gave them a gentle squeeze. "But we're going to find him. Don't worry."

She opened her mouth, but he cut her off. "And by 'we' I mean the police. Just so we're clear."

"I found him the last time."

"Don't remind me. I'll follow you to school. I'll come in and make sure he's not holed up in the building. We'll go from there."

She itched to smooth out the worry lines etched into his forehead, so she agreed. "I'll grab my school bag and meet you out front."

"Key." He held out a hand.

She raised her eyebrows.

"I need a key so I can let in the guy installing the security alarm."

"Fine." She fished a spare key out of a drawer and tossed it to him. "How am I supposed to know how this thing works?"

He snatched the key out of the air. "I'll come over later and show you how to use the security system."

"I have a couple of meetings after school. I won't be home until late, so I'll come over for my key when I'm done." She glanced at her watch. "We'd better go."

The sky opened up as soon as they stepped out of the door. Normally, she'd take a minute to inhale the scent of the rain, but Chase was already halfway to his vehicle. She clutched her bag and purse close as she sprinted to her car.

She tried to see past the frenetic pace of the windshield wipers. Everything appeared normal at first until he changed course and went left after she turned right.

Her cell phone rang and she picked it up and hit *talk*.

"Don't stop. Keep going." The line went dead.

Um? And just how was she supposed to do that? Before she could decide, her phone rang again. She rolled her eyes before answering.

"Hello?"

"Ms. Wheeler? It's me."

"Jason? Thank goodness." Her fingers tightened around the steering wheel at the whispered sound of his voice. She checked the rearview mirror as she parked by the curb.

"Yeah, it's me."

"Where are you? Are you all right?" He sounded

out of breath. Rushed. Scared.

"I'm at home. I need help with something."

"I'm thirty seconds away, Jason. Hold on tight. Do. Not. Move."

"No, I—"

Lily cringed as a massive bang echoed in her ear. "Jason?"

"I gotta go."

The line went dead.

"Wait. No." Her eyes darted every direction, as if that would help her figure out what the heck had just happened. No time to ponder the possibilities. Her heart constricting, she yelled his name into her phone, "Jason!"

Two seconds after she got no response, she was dialing nine-one-one.

One second after placing her emergency call, she was cranking her car around and heading in the opposite direction.

Through the driving rain, she picked out Chase's police cruiser, the wide open door to the McCarran's house. Her foot hit the brake at the sight of the smaller body on the ground and the much bigger one guarding it. Without thinking, she opened her car door and got out. Chase shouted something to her, but the only thing she saw was Jason. She swiped at water pouring over her face.

Was that blood?

Halfway across the road, the heels of her sandals skidded on the wet pavement. Balance lost, her knees slammed against the cold wet road. Again, Chase yelled out, but the thunder of blood pumping in her ears made it impossible to catch what he said. She got to her feet in time to see Chase prop Jason up into a half sitting position, his body between the boy and the open door.

Chase's head whipped up, and he motioned for her to go back. Her legs refused to cooperate. They were exposed, nothing but flat ground between Chase, who was shielding Jason, and anyone wanting to hurt them. The door behind them stood wide open. She pushed at the wet tendrils of hair hanging in her face. Sirens sounded in the background, and her head swung toward the sound.

The patrol car arrived in a river of rain, and Mike bolted from the vehicle. Chase hollered something to Mike, but she couldn't hear. She watched Chase hold his position as Mike rushed up. Watched as Mike positioned himself beside the open doorway, watched him disappear through it.

She jolted when someone tapped her on the shoulder. Stan Knight asked if she was okay. It shook her loose. She scrambled toward the pair, only to be held back by a hand on her arm.

"He needs you to stay here." Through the slashing rain, she saw Stan shake his head. "Let him do his job."

Mike exited the house and hunkered down beside Chase. Chase motioned her forward after what seemed like hours, but was really minutes. She reached him as he put a restraining hand on Jason's shoulder.

"Don't move for a bit yet." To her, he asked, "Are you okay?" He peered through the rain as if trying to discern the truth for himself.

She waved his concern away. "Yes. How's Jason?"

"He's fine. More shaken up than anything. A bloody nose."

"What happened?"

She glanced at Jason. "Are you okay?"

"I'm fine." Jason lifted a hand to his head, pulled it away, and grimaced as the rain washed the blood off his fingers.

Chase gave him a look. "He thought he heard a noise. Made a run for it and tripped."

She pushed her hands through her wet hair as relief loosened her muscles. "He did hear a noise. I heard it, too. He phoned my cell. Are you sure no one's in the house?" Jason slumped against Chase. "We should get him out of the rain."

"Yeah. I'm taking him with me." Jason didn't argue with the help to get him to his feet, just held on tighter to his backpack. He left Jason with Mike to pull her aside. "I need you to do me a favor. Don't go home."

She frowned down at her soaked clothing. "I have to change. I have to go home."

"Go to Kate's. Go anywhere, but promise me you won't go home."

"All right. I promise." She squeezed the hand resting on her arm. She willed him to believe her.

He waved Stan over. "Can you stick with her and make sure she gets where she needs to go and then into the school?"

"No problem."

"Thanks." He didn't let go. The accompanying intensity in his eyes backed up his next request. "Call me when you're done at work and I'll come and get you."

"Okay." He looked worried. Like the ante had been upped. They were running out of time.

She climbed into her vehicle, tried to see past the rain, but all she saw was Chase putting himself between an open doorway and a child.

****

The day got worse as it crawled along, and by worse, she meant curse worthy. Her twenty-four hour deadline was up. She had nothing to give Raphael Tessier. Stupid or not, she refused to be used or intimidated. They would figure something out.

Chase phoned the office of the school late in the day to say he couldn't pick her up as previously arranged. Instead, he insisted someone else be available to walk her out to her car when she finished, which put Principal Amanda Henry in a superior snit as she wasn't Lily's social secretary. A fact she made sure to remind Lily of every time she caught her in the hallway. Plus, she'd finally connected the name, Chase Porter, to her former least favorite student. She'd taken it out on Lily. Now, at the end of the day, the only other person left in the school was the janitor, who had scared her senseless as she rounded a corner. Her heart rate still hadn't returned to normal.

She wanted to go home. To Chase. To her bed. To Chase in her bed. She imagined all kinds of lovely scenarios while Amanda slapped papers around on her desk, wielding her stapler like she wished it were a nail gun and Chase was the paper. She might have even smiled once. That smile was almost as scary as Raphael Tessier's.

Tired of waiting for her escort, Lily paced the hallway and prayed for deliverance. Five minutes later, she checked her watch, then dug out her cell phone.

"Chase, it's Lily."

"What's up?"

She lowered her voice for no good reason. "I'm still here. With Amanda. You remember Ms. Henry don't you? Because she remembers you, and she's taking it out on me."

"Sorry. Things are kind of crazy."

"I need to get out of here."

"Just a few more—"

"Now."

"Give me a minute to call Stan, and I'll have him take you to my place."

"Stan? Knight? What's he got to do with all this? Isn't he retired? And wasn't he at Jason's house this morning?"

There was a pause, a quick conversation with someone in the background. He sighed, "Look, I'll explain later."

"Fine, later. I'm more concerned with now. Chase, I can get myself from the school to your house without the sky falling. I'll have Amanda walk out with me, she'd scare the devil away."

"I don't like it."

Of course, he didn't. "It'll be fine. I promise."

"Okay. I'm on my way back in. I'll be there in ten. Don't do anything reckless."

"Who? Me?" She hit *end* and went to give her boss the good news.

She dragged Amanda with her out to her car, but not before she'd made Lily wait another twenty minutes. Lily resisted the urge to run her down as Amanda walked away. Barely. At least the rain had stopped mid-afternoon. Head full of worry over Jason, Chase, doing her job and with her eyes busy searching the street for anything out of the ordinary; she parked in front of her house and headed in the direction of Chase's.

She kept her eyes wide open, shot a quick glance at the few cars dotting the street and parked in private driveways. A huge construction-sized waste bin sat across the street, but the workers had long since gone. Everything was quiet.

Another meeting with Mike and Jason's Student Services worker over the lunch hour had produced a measure of reassurance. By now, Jason and his aunt were on their way out of town for an undisclosed amount of time. She wasn't privy to the details. But just knowing he was out of Raphael Tessier's reach eased some of the ache from her back and shoulder muscles. There wasn't much more she could do to help Jason. He was as safe as they could make him. The only thing she needed to do was forward his school work to his case worker.

She gathered the edges of her borrowed leather jacket, hugged them close against the cool temperature. Jason was safe. Her twenty-four hours were up, but she was still standing. She'd given Chase a call to tell him she was almost there. On the whole, she was feeling pretty proud of how she'd covered all her bases.

Something flashed to the right of her, and she frowned. A second later, an arm wrapped around her throat, pulled her over to the curb, toward the approaching car. She gargled out a few weak cries as her arms flailed and her heels scraped over the hard concrete of the sidewalk. She battered her hands against anything she could reach and managed one good scream.

"Shut up." The familiar low voice and the overpowering sweet scent of his cologne initiated her gag reflex.

Then everything happened so fast, she could only process flashes. Her name, a shout in the distance. The suffocating upholstery of the backseat. Her face pressed against it. The smell. The car jerked forward as Raphael Tessier vaulted in and landed on top of her. The air left her lungs in one great whoosh.

Could. Not. Breathe.

In desperation, she reared up and smashed the back of her head against his face.

Things slid downhill at race car speed after a small popping sound echoed in her ear. A large hand pushed her face back down into the reeking upholstery. Panic, combined with the threat of suffocation, had her twisting and reaching for anything to grab or pull. It was a relief when he grasped a fist full of her hair and yanked her head up. She sucked in air, clutching for something solid as the car fishtailed around a corner on squealing tires.

Terror eroded away any thoughts of self-defense, and the knife at her throat paralyzed her, fingertips to toes.

"Sit up."

She hesitated, the knife bit into her skin. His grip tightened on her scalp, and she cried out as he ripped out strands of hair.

"Get up."

"Then get off me."

"Move." He let go, and she closed her eyes in relief. Terrified and silent, she scrambled back into the corner. The knife was in his hand, impossibly sharp and long.

"You bitch." He swiped at the blood pouring from his nose. It smeared across his web tattoo, and she shuddered. Then they were all struggling to keep upright after a sharp swerve around another corner.

She'd never seen a deader pair of eyes. Blank, even with blood pouring out of his nose. He swiped at his nose again, sneered at the back of his hand. The knife lowered, instead of feeling relieved, she shrank back.

His backhand caught her across her right cheekbone. "That's for not taking my request seriously."

Pain exploded under her eye. It paralyzed her. Fed her rising panic. She tried to shuffle her way further back into the corner. A few scant inches. Not enough space, not enough time to think. He grabbed her wrist and jerked. She struggled to find the door handle with her other hand. Her fingers closed around it, and she heaved with all her might, the useless clicks echoing in the small space. The corner of his lips curled the tiniest bit.

"Pull harder. Fight it. Scream for it, little teacher." He leaned forward until all she could see were his black, pit-like pupils. The knife disappeared as he caught hold of her chin. The other hand pushed at the hem of her T-shirt.

"This is for breaking my fucking nose." Horror spurted out of her like a geyser as his hand strained upward. Panic raised her fists, mobilized her feet, and snapped her teeth. The fight got nasty at the speed of light for all of five seconds.

"One more move, and I'll make your dead body the kid's final warning."

Her breath heaved in and out. The effort hurt. Her throat clogged, her mind a useless mash of fear and pain.

"Where. Is. He?" Tessier demanded.

She shook her head, wanted to scream at him to go to hell. She wanted so much to be heroic, but she was so scared it numbed her vocal cords.

His fingers carved deeper into her skin.

"I don't know." She closed her eyes and thanked God it was true. He could do whatever he wanted to her, she couldn't tell him anything. The thought gave her a kernel of courage.

"I swear. I don't know." It came up as a whisper, not the confident retort she'd imagined, but it came out.

"Did you get what I asked for?"

She tried to look away, but his fingers pulled her back.

"I want what's mine." He paused, his hand on her breast. As he squeezed and twisted, something ugly spread across his face. Sick pleasure. His fingers squashed harder. "You understand me? People are going to die if I don't get back what's mine."

She slapped at his hand, tried not to let terror guide her, but she was no David and her Goliath knew it. Every muscle convulsed when he slid the knife under her shirt and sliced it open. Frantic, dry sobs birthed out of her.

The car swerved, and the driver's voice cut through. "Spider, we got trouble."

Raphael Tessier hissed.

Lily prayed.

He yanked a small cell phone out of nowhere and tucked it into her jacket pocket. "I'm giving you one more chance. Forty-eight hours. Or someone in this town dies. That cop of yours can't protect everyone. I'll be in touch. Don't do anything stupid." To the driver, he said, "Unlock the doors."

The clunk of the locks opening echoed in the small space. She searched for the knife, but couldn't see it.

"Open the door." He stared at her with those eyes, and there was nothing. Absolutely nothing there.

The night whizzed past the window, shadow shapes spinning and disappearing. She didn't move.

"Open it."

Escape, even when offered, had her shaking her head. Too fast. They were going too fast. His hand snaked past her. She grabbed for it, but missed as the car braked then swerved. The car door flew open on the first yank, and wind whipped into the car.

She bounced once, twice. Gravel bit into her back as she skidded across the road. Lights flashed and more gravel flew as another vehicle attempted to brake. She curled into herself and braced for the worst.

****

Chase vaulted out of his truck and scrambled across the wet gravel, stones spraying in every direction as he dropped down next to Lily's prone body.

"Lily!" *Please, God, please, God, PLEASE, GOD.*

He lifted a shaking hand, then hesitated before gently placing it on the back of her head. He pulled it back, sticky with blood. She was breathing. He was beyond thankful.

The murmurs slipped out of him—love words, promises, and crumbs of the past. She twisted toward him, and he gulped in his first deep breath in ten torturous minutes.

"Chase?"

"I'm here, baby." He brushed back curls and half-heartedly tried to stop her when she attempted to sit up. He gave up and held on for dear life as tenderly as he could manage.

Her whole body shuddered as her arms banded around his neck. Her hot tears sliced at his heart. He held on tighter. The first patrol car reached them. The door slammed, and Mike scrambled into his line of vision.

"I'll call for an ambulance." Chase managed a nod as Mike radioed for help.

Lily shivered, and he had to press closer to hear her. "Don't leave me. Come with me."

"Baby, I couldn't let go if I tried." He tucked her in and stared off into the dark. It was going to take the rest of his life to recover from this.

He shifted his weight, searched the road for the lights of the ambulance. He heard it before he saw it. He smoothed a hand over her matted curls.

"I've got you." He placed a kiss near her ear. "I've got you."

Chapter Eleven

Lily averted her gaze from the sidewalk and focused on Chase unlocking her door. She remained vertical by sheer force of will, desperate to get inside. Even with Chase and Mike stuck to her like burrs, the whispering breeze carried threats. The shadows hid monsters threatening to break through their guard. Paranoia bloomed.

Yesterday's Lily welcomed new challenges, never gave up, never doubted her own sense of security. Today's Lily hugged the paranoia close. Embraced it. Sanctioned its hardwiring. She slipped through the door the second it swung open.

Chase and Mike moved in behind her as she headed for the kitchen with its potpourri of ripening tomatoes, fresh cut daisies, and shuttered windows. She hugged the scent of the familiar close. Normal—she craved it. Prayed for it. On autopilot, she reached over and tapped the message button on her answering machine, thinking Kate had returned the call she'd made from the hospital.

"Sweet dreams, little teacher."

Invaded. He was here, too. He was everywhere. She slapped bandaged hands over her buzzing ears to block out the sound of his voice and his list of horrors. The room started to spin. The wall braced her back as she shrank against it.

The hint of muffled words slipped in through her fingers, and Chase appeared, worry etching harsh lines across his forehead, around his mouth. "Lily. It's okay, baby. He's not here. He's long gone. Listen to me."

He shushed her. Whispered and crooned to her, his hands on her face. She leaned her head back against the wall and slid down, embarrassment, coupled with exhaustion, dropping her to the floor.

His face appeared in front of hers. From his haunches, gentle hands covered hers and pried them loose from her ears. He gathered them into his, massaging her fingers, bypassing the scrapes gouged into her palms. She curled her fingers around his.

"You're safe here, baby." His hands coaxed her body upward. She stepped into him and dropped her head against his wide chest, scented with sweat and something only Chase possessed. His breath brushed her cheek as he murmured against her ear. "It's okay. It's going to be okay. He's not going to hurt you again."

How long they remained entwined she didn't know, and she didn't care. He offered a sense of security she'd feared lost forever. She was staying put until she was warm enough to pull away or the world ended, whichever came first. She heard them talking over her and concentrated on the warm hands rubbing her back. Heard the coffeepot start to drip, the aroma registering, along with other trivialities—a cupboard door opening, the fridge, the scrape of a chair. She lifted her head. Let Chase coax her in the direction of a chair.

"Here, have a seat. Let's get you comfortable." A blanket appeared, and he wrapped it around her.

She pulled the warm fleece closer. "I'm sorry."

"You've got nothing to be sorry about." He dropped into one of the other chairs while Mike placed a cup of coffee in front of her.

She ignored it. "I should have parked at your house. I didn't think—"

"Don't." He leaned over and brushed his thumbs over her cheeks. "It's not your fault."

"I know." She shut her eyes, but she knew it wasn't true. She nodded to appease them, too tired to argue.

"Are you up for talking to Mike? It'll only take a few minutes."

Fifteen minutes later, she insisted she had nothing more to add and announced she was desperate to clean up. She left them to talk or strategize or whatever it was they did. The stench of fear still lingered, and she wanted rid of it. In the bathroom, she pulled off the scrubs they'd given her to wear at the hospital. Bandages and skin adhesive made showering impossible, so she settled for washing her hair in the sink and made do with a sponge bath to get rid of the worst of the stench.

In the quiet sanctuary of her bedroom, she climbed into some baggy pajamas. Not ready to face the world, but composed enough to face her rescuers. She stepped into the hallway as the front door closed. More whispers, then the lock clicked and the alarm beeped. She hated that she hesitated.

Intellectually, she knew she was safe, but it didn't help her limbs to move or keep her from imagining the worst. She listened to the rustle of footsteps. Chase rounded the corner, stopping short at the sight of her. Vanity pulled a hand to her hair, to the damp, messy curls. Insecurity took over, she shrank inside her comfy nightwear, her hand settling over the small bandage at her throat.

"I'm going to stay here tonight." His hand ploughed through hair already standing out at odd angles. An overnight bag he must have slipped out to get gripped in his hand. Even at this distance, she saw his Adam's apple bob as he swallowed. "If that's okay with you?"

She nodded.

He lifted his bag. “Mind if I have a shower?”

“No. Go ahead.” Relief washed over her as she nodded. She needed him to keep the bogeyman locked out of her brain.

****

The mattress dipped as Chase shifted position for the hundredth time. The very last place on earth he wanted to be was here. The last thing he wanted to do was leave. He should be out there tracking down Raphael Tessier. So why this overwhelming urge to stay? Forever. The battle had been going on all night. Stay or go. Careful to move nice and slow, he swung his feet to the floor. He scrubbed his hands over his face before resting his elbows on his knees and letting his head drop.

Visualizing Raphael Tessier broken, ripped to shreds, his head on a pike had wasted away the first hour. Thoughts and memories of his dead partner had overtaken the second hour. He’d relived the night in the alley, his hands pressed against Conrad’s stomach. Trying to staunch the flow of blood, knowing it wouldn’t do a thing considering the hole in his skull. Waiting for help, for a bullet in his back, while the life pumped out of his best friend.

During the last hour, more memories flayed him to bits. Of the soul sucking days he’d spent after leaving Aspen Lake. Of trying to forget. Reliving the one memory he avoided like the plague. Of his last night here. Of the next morning. The confrontation with his father. Bruised knuckles, bruised face, bruised soul.

Hoping for clarity, he ground the heels of his palms into his eyelids. He needed a cup of strong, black coffee. One quick glance over his shoulder told him that wasn’t happening any time soon. The sheets twisted tight under her hands, and his name drifted out on a whisper from the pillow she strangled in her sleep. He sank back down onto the mattress and reached over to stroke her hair.

"Lily. Baby, wake up. You're dreaming." He spread her hair out behind her on the pillow. The soft strands clung to his fingers.

Her body jolted and braced for impact. He smoothed a hand over her shoulder, down her arm, to her hand still clutching her pillow. He rubbed his thumb over her knuckles, massaging out the tension. "Shush, you're okay. It's me."

"Chase?"

"Yeah, and you're safe in bed. Go back to sleep." Her hand trembled the tiniest bit under his. He resisted the urge to squeeze tighter. In the dark of the half-moon light, tucked up under the bed sheet, she looked very breakable, like those fancy designer eggs he'd heard about long ago. Fragile as glass.

"In a bit." Her knees came up as she pushed up from the bed and wrapped her arms around them. She pressed a cheek against her knees.

"Bad one?" He ran a gentle hand over her back, careful to skim over the bandages. Scrapes and bruises only. She'd gotten off lucky according to the doctor. But it changed a person. Violence did that, scraped off the soft flesh of innocence and shored up new layers in its place. Inside and out.

"Yeah." Her shoulders sagged.

"Can I get you anything? Glass of water, something to eat?" He grimaced.

"No, I'm fine." She lifted her head.

"You're fine," he repeated. That made one of them. Not that he believed her.

"Well, I will be soon enough." She brushed a hand over his hair and down his cheek. "I'm not going to give him the satisfaction of being anything other than fine."

"Good to know." *He* was never going to be fine again. *He* would see her being dragged into that car for all eternity. Sprawled across the gravel until time stopped.

Her bandaged hand slipped to his chest and she sighed, low and deep. "You're so warm."

He stilled her hand. "You should try and get some sleep."

"I don't need sleep," she whispered. The little bit of moonlight glimmered off her curls. "I need you to warm me up."

"Okay." He prepared to tuck her back into the blankets.

"Not that kind of warm. Alive. Warm."

"I don't think that's a good idea." More like a crappy idea. But his body reacted, every muscle contracting at the chance to channel his leftover adrenalin somewhere.

Yes, very bad idea. She was ready to shatter into a million pieces. Her body and mind wanted warmth, comfort, to forget. His begged for action, for war, for salvation.

"I think it is." She shoved the sheet aside and crawled over top of him.

Damn it to hell, the whole situation had "worst decision ever" written all over it. Too emotional. Too close. Sure enough, he ended up in exactly the wrong place, between her legs, winded and hostage to cravings he couldn't control. Her hands exploring his jean clad hips and her lips warm against his T-shirt covered stomach. His muscles jerked in response, every functioning brain cell surfing the wave of lust rushing to his cock. She was plastered over him like wet paint, and he was the hard, weather-battered board desperate to soak it up. Every millimeter of skin reacted, every hair follicle anticipated, and every drop of blood pumping through the chambers of his heart waited for the slide of her tongue, the grasp of her fingers, or the clench of her thighs. He didn't care which came first, as long as it was now. He filled his hands with fistfuls of sweet smelling sheets and knew the second her lips curved into a winning smile.

A shred of sanity. *Wrong to take advantage.* She was afraid and scared. But his shirt was coming up, and his hands let of go of the sheets to help finish the job. He tried to anchor his back to the bed while her hands and lips traveled across his pecs. Breathed in deep as her tongue lapped at his skin, while her hips settled into position.

He inhaled the scent of her shampoo. Took one last stab at honorable.

"Not a good idea." Except it came out garbled and lacking the "not" part.

"Very good idea." Her palms came to rest on either side of him, and she leaned down and kissed him.

The air purged from his chest on a soft whoosh. His lungs stuttered, than stalled when her lips ripped away from his to travel the sensitive skin of his quaking stomach muscles.

"Lower." The word parachuted out on a moan as his vision blurred. He wanted this so bad. He prayed for it. And it made him feel like a total shit for not stopping her before her lips kissed his zipper. Then his hips lifted and his back arched off the bed.

Why were his pants still on? He'd worn them to bed for a reason. Hadn't he? He couldn't breathe with his pants on.

And, like wishing made it so, her talented hands unbuttoned, unzipped, and undressed. He ground his teeth together, ignored his cock's happy dance and made a grab for her hands, because he needed to do something about her pajamas. He needed to put his hands on bare skin. But he had no idea how to navigate her map of bruises and scrapes without causing her pain. She read his mind and twisted and shimmied until her skin glistened in the low light of the moon.

His toes curled into the sheets. Her hand pressed against his inner thigh while her mouth suckled and lapped and savored. The next thing he knew, her vagina was doing a slow slide over his straining erection, and it greased a fire that had suffered from not enough fuel for ten long years.

He forgot…everything. His hands went from tearing at the sheets to skimming over smooth skin, finding breasts to fill his hands, dewy skin to quench his thirst, and a hot heat to arch against, over and over again. His thighs went to work underneath her until she slapped her hands onto his chest, her nails dug in, and his back arched off the bed in a final thrust.

It wasn't until she collapsed on top of him that he realized they hadn't used a condom.

****

She let the thunder beat of his heart lull her into a half-sleep. Her eyes refused to open when he shifted beneath her.

"Have to sleep on my stomach tonight," she muttered.

Whispered cuss words registered in the back of her mind, but she chose to ignore them. Instead, she groaned and tried to find a comfortable spot. She hated sleeping on her stomach, but the abrasions on her back made it a necessary evil. The bed shifted and she reached out to Chase.

"Stay."

The mattress dipped and the covers came to rest at her waist with only the sheet left to cover her wounded back. She doubted he'd appreciate her thanks. His hand brushed her hair and she let the drugging afterglow of sex pull her toward sleep.

The next time she opened her eyes, the pale light of dawn showed through the blinds. A full body ache reminded her. The bandage covering the cut on her throat was stiff and uncomfortable. But it could have been so much worse. She offered up a prayer of thanks to Kate for insisting she take the leather jacket. It had saved her back from being torn to shreds.

She wrapped the sheet around her naked body and struggled to sit up, listened for Chase and heard running water in the background.

Sex was great therapy. No sleeping pill or pain pill could have accomplished the same level of oblivion as great sex. In the bathroom, the shower shut off. The sex had distracted her. Allowed her to forget. She'd also used it as a license to take what she wanted. Now was all she had, and time was running out on tomorrow.

She bit her lip on hearing the bathroom door open, and she listened for the direction his footsteps would take. She lifted her head at the exact moment Chase paused in the doorway.

She smiled at the sight of him wrapped in a fuzzy pink towel, a dozen or so stray drops of water drizzling down from his hair, over his shoulders. His Saint Thomas of Aquinas medal hanging around his neck. She remembered him telling her the medal was one of the last things his mother had given him. It was the only thing he had left of her besides one photograph. He never took it off.

An itch developed in the dead center of her palm as a drop of water slid down the middle of his chest. She rubbed her hand against the sheets.

"You're awake."

"Just." She decided to go for broke and held out her hand. He crossed the room, took it, and perched on the edge of the bed.

She looked into those eyes, so serious, so haunted. "Thank you for everything. I know I haven't been as cooperative as I needed to be, but I promise from now on not to be stupid, or blasé, or difficult. If I can help it." She held up two fingers of her right hand and used them to cross her heart.

He'd kept hold of her other hand, and his thumb started making slow circles against her palm. "Don't."

She frowned. "Don't what?"

"Don't thank me." The other hand came up to rest against her cheek, and his eyes locked onto hers, and her heart stuttered. "And don't make this into something more than it is. All I ever wanted was for you to be safe. I should have stayed away. Kept my promise."

She didn't understand. "Stayed away? Kept your promise?"

"I never wanted you to get hurt."

She tilted her head to the side to get closer to his hand and the fading warmth, to grasp a bit of it and keep it close. "It's not your fault."

"Yes, it is. I let you down last night. You could have been killed. I didn't have the sense to use a condom last night. I'm screwing up your life. I never wanted that to happen. Not then and not now."

"What? You're not making any sense." She smoothed a hand over his hair. "Let's deal with the last issue first. I'm on the pill, so that point is moot. And Raphael Tessier is responsible for last night. But I don't understand. You left to keep me safe? Where's that coming from? What promise?"

"Ridding the earth of scum like Raphael Tessier is my job."

"But the sole responsibility for it does not rest on your shoulders."

His hands dropped. "Did you know he beat his pregnant girlfriend to death?"

She hadn't, and she wasn't sure she wanted to know it now.

"He's dead inside that body. He doesn't have a conscience. Like his brother and his father before him. Violence is in his blood. Some of us are built like that, hardwired for it."

Her eyebrows shot straight up. "Some of us? Meaning you. You're comparing yourself to Raphael Tessier? To a gang member? A terrorist? A murderer?"

"Not to that extreme. But to what links us. Yes." He didn't so much a blink. He was dead serious. She sat back, dazed.

"That's ridiculous." The very idea repulsed her, chilled her skin, made it crawl.

"And denial's never solved anything."

"That still doesn't explain why you said you left to keep me safe."

"I didn't want to wake up one morning and look into your bruised face and know I put those bruises there."

She stared at him, and then she couldn't help it, she laughed. "Oh, please, that would never happen."

He pushed off from the bed and paced to the window.

She frowned as she gathered up the sheet and went after him. "That is the single most preposterous thing I've ever heard. You would never hurt me." But he had. Not in the way he meant. He never would, but he had bruised her heart, and there was every chance he'd do it again. "Listen to me. You are nothing like your father."

He spun around. "How do you know that? What factual evidence are you basing that assumption on?"

She grabbed his arm. "I know it. In here." She pressed her palm to her heart.

"You don't know anything about the last ten years or what I've done."

"I know you put yourself through school with no help from anyone. I know you've made a reputation for yourself as a cop who gets the job done. I know you care—"

"I chose a career and a place other than this town to call my own. That will never change. Not today and not tomorrow. I don't want to care about this place. I don't want to remember whose blood runs through these veins." He wrapped strong fingers around hers, the ones with a death grip on his arm.

"Then I'll remember for you. Yours." She grasped his medal. "And your mother's."

He stopped her. "Don't fool yourself. If it's in there, there's only a trace amount."

He peeled her fingers off his medal, folded them over into his hand, squeezed, and then he let go. "Why don't you get dressed? I'll go make coffee. And we'll decide where we go from here."

She watched him exit the room before turning back to the window. She nudged the blind slats apart and stared out. Where else could they go from here? Except toward the end. He was going to get there before her. But that didn't mean she had to make it easy for him.

Chapter Twelve

Chase waited until he heard the water running in the bathroom before pulling out his phone and punching in numbers. He was beginning to feel next to useless, handcuffed by *feelings*. Flash images from the night before sparked into his tired brain. Lily struggling. The car door closing behind her. The sensation of standing still even though he was moving. A car door swinging open. A body in the headlights.

Raphael Tessier didn't make idle threats. Chase *had* to find him first. Before he carried out his depraved promises of last night. Tessier was desperate and desperate people did dangerous, stupid things. Made mistakes. Did things that couldn't be undone or stitched up——just buried.

Chase hit the last number in the sequence connecting him to a former colleague from the Combined Forces Special Enforcement Unit. He had dialed the number umpteen times in the last few days, checking on the information his contact was gathering. The CFSEU was a joint effort between the RCMP and different police departments. They targeted organized criminal activity, and they were the experts. They knew their stuff.

It was a short conversation. They were still looking for Kevin McCarran. The Prairie Brotherhood was still eager to find him. Surprise, surprise. Weren't they all?

He hung up and looked around for something that would keep his hands busy. He settled on food. He cracked a couple of eggs into a pan and dumped a couple of slices of bread into the toaster. He wasn't much of a cook, but Lily needed to eat. They both did. He dug cheese out of the fridge, poured some kind of sorry excuse for juice into a glass, and arranged the offering on the table.

She wandered in looking more than exhausted around the edges. She looked wary and with good reason. The sight of her bandaged hands and throat shot jabs of steadfastness straight to his heart. He'd do anything to protect her. RT wasn't the only one getting desperate. Problem was, he couldn't afford to make any more mistakes. Not where Lily was concerned.

"Coffee?"

"Yes, please."

He set a mug down and pulled out the chair across from her. Sitting here all cozy, together like a couple, made him twitchy. She sipped at the coffee and hummed in appreciation. Together, like this, could become a habit. It would be so easy.

"I phoned and arranged to take some time off work." Her fingers swiped at some crumbs caught at the corner of her mouth. His mind wandered. He snapped it back. When had this become a good thing? A sexy thing? Staying over and eating breakfast with someone?

"Great." He picked up his coffee and gulped half of it down.

"So, what's the plan? Where do we start?"

He shook his head. "I'm going to work. You are staying here, doors locked, alarm set, and patrols coming by every half hour or so, and me on speed dial."

She sighed and leaned back. She winced and straightened back up. "Fine. In fact, I'm more than okay with the idea."

Concern and guilt shot through him. "Are you sure you're okay?"

"Yes, no need to fuss." She sighed over another sip of coffee. "I wish we knew what you were looking for."

"We're narrowing it down." They were getting closer to figuring out how tight Kevin McCarran's connection was to the Prairie Brotherhood. He had to have passed something on to his brother. Something Raphael Tessier was desperate to get back. Money, drugs, names?

"Well, I hope we figure it out soon."

So did he. He shoved a portion of toast in his mouth, took a quick swallow of coffee, and stood. "I'm going to try and reach Jason later this morning."

"Be safe." She lifted her face up for what only could be a kiss. Very homey, very every day.

"Always." He squirmed a bit, schooled his features into an accommodating mask, dipped his head for a quick kiss.

She snagged his shirtfront. "We're going to talk again later. Because I'm not satisfied with that quaint little conversation we had in my bedroom, so don't for one minute think that was the end of it. We're not kids anymore. You don't get to make all the decisions. I know you don't want me to get the wrong idea, to assume things about the future. I know you're scared, and that you don't want to hear that either. You want me to trust you. But you have to be open to trusting me, too. "

Her fingers unraveled from his shirt, and she sat back, determination written all over her face.

He did the only thing he could do, he left. Half an hour later, he stalked into the detachment and headed for Mike's desk, locked, loaded and prepared to take his shitty mood out on him.

"Got anything?"

"And good morning to you, too. I'm fine. A little tired, but what can you do?" Mike shrugged and leaned back in his chair.

"My apologies for not inquiring after your state of well-being." Chase put his hands on his hips. "Now. Got anything?"

Mike reached for a folder and handed it to Chase. "For what it's worth."

He flipped it open and frowned at the stack of messages.

Mike grinned. "Those are helpful 'tips' that have been phoned in so far."

Chase thumbed through the stack. "Any chance one or two of these might actually be useful?"

"Bernice put the ones on top that sounded promising." Mike tapped the first one. "This one's from Ken Sheppard. He and his wife have a farm north of town, about twenty minutes out. He's not the sort to call in unless he felt sure something wasn't right. There's a couple more that might be useful."

"It's a place to start." And gave him something else to concentrate on besides Lily and their upcoming talk. He'd said all he had to say. Now was the time for action. To get things done. Any other plans she had would have to wait.

Ken Sheppard was waiting for them at the front door of his ranch style house. After a brief discussion they followed his directions to an old abandoned farmyard situated down the road a couple of miles.

Chase exited the cruiser, along with Mike. He surveyed the broken-down house with the peeling paint, the hanging-by-a-thread shutters framing the filthy, dirt smudged windows. He glanced across the hood at Mike.

"No vehicles in sight."

Mike shrugged. "The vehicle they had last night

was stolen. No big surprise. We came across it on the opposite side of town. Someone's going over it now."

Chase hunched down beside some tire tracks. "A lot of tracks for an abandoned yard." Straightening up, he eyed the windows again.

"Could be kids using it as a party house."

Chase scanned the yard. "Let's see if anyone's currently in residence." He drew his gun. Mike did the same. One hefty shove, and the rotted door swung open. They weren't two feet inside the door when the rev of a motorbike sounded from outside. Chase signaled to Mike, and they slipped back out the front door in time to see the dirt bike disappear down a rutted track toward a grove of trees at the back of the property.

"Shit." As Mike radioed in the information on the bike and its rider, Chase searched the horizon.

"Any idea where that trail leads?" He dipped his head in the direction of the grove of trees.

"None. But Ken Sheppard rents the surrounding land, and he might."

While relaying information, they did a check of the rest of the house. There wasn't much to see. Garbage littered the floor—fast food wrappers, pop cans, beer cans. He kicked at a bundle of rope and a roll of duct tape.

"They were probably planning on bringing the kid here."

Mike began opening and shutting cupboard doors in the kitchen. "These guys are starting to piss me off."

Chase grunted.

"I'm glad Jason's aunt is getting temporary guardianship. You ask me, the kid deserves someone who is going to look after him."

Chase frowned at the back of Mike's head. "The kid could definitely use a break."

"You know Lily, once she gets an idea in her

head there's no stopping her." He slammed a cupboard shut. "And when she decides to do something…"

"Yeah." He was only just realizing. He righted an old wooden chair. Chase stared out a window and off in the direction of the dirt bike. He shook his head, then looked back at Mike. "We're missing something."

Mike rubbed a hand over his face. "We'll figure it out."

"We'd better."

"We're all functioning on about three hours sleep. But even sleep deprived we're smarter than this son of a bitch."

Chase nodded out of habit.

"We're going to catch these scum before they hurt anyone else."

Chase opened his mouth, and then shut it again without uttering a word. They exited the house and ended up back on the weed infested front lawn. A soft clang echoed in the still air. He cocked his head to the north in the direction of the rundown shed twenty feet back from the house. The clang sounded again.

Chase rested his hand on top of his pistol. The small shed sported a shiny new lock and lengths of chain. They inspected the perimeter of the shed, checking for trip wires or traps. Chase pointed to a jumble of antifreeze and drain cleaner containers lying in a heap a couple feet away from the back of the shack.

Mike ran a hand through his hair. "I'll get the bolt cutters."

"Could this whole thing be about drugs? Could it be that simple?" Chase bent down and grabbed up a fist full of dry gray dirt, and then let it sift through his fingers.

"You don't believe that any more than I do."

Mike made short work of the lock and the length of chain snaked to the ground. The double shed doors swung wide open to reveal dirty coffee filters, plastic bottles, a hot plate, and enough chemicals to cook a couple of batches of meth, or crank.

Chase, straightened, whistled, and reached out a hand to silence the ancient chimes dangling from the roof overhang. "They aren't going to be happy about losing this cache."

Mike nodded in the direction of the trail. "My guess is the chef went that direction."

"For his sake, I hope we catch him first."

****

Lily glared at the pile of student assignments she had yet to grade. Frustration and an inability to concentrate made her grouchy. Nothing was getting past the fear. She shrank back against the couch, but the pain from her abrasions pushed her forward. The handy little bottle of pills sat on the coffee table in front of her. Too bad it didn't dull her mental aches and pains. Darkness threatened to descend soon. It made coping so much harder.

Her ears picked up the sound of a vehicle motor shutting off and a door slamming. She tensed. Knowing who had arrived didn't help. Her body braced as her hands clenched. He'd beaten tracks for the door fast enough this morning, but at least he'd come back.

She pushed up from the couch and went to the window. Parting the blinds, she watched him stop to talk to the departing cop. Learning his moves was becoming one of her favorite pastimes. Back straight, face somber. His hands went to his hips, and her lips curved, he was all business, no nonsense. She thought of last night, how she'd taken what she'd wanted, the rush of pleasure, and heat bloomed under her skin. She patted her cheeks. Her lips tingled, remembering how his skin felt beneath the tips of her fingers, the sound that started deep in his throat and poured out of him as her body slid over his.

She didn't move when he rang the bell. She stayed put when he opened the door and punched in her code, but her thighs clenched when he called her name. Her fingertips curled into her palms as he came around the corner.

They eyed each other.

"Hey. You okay?"

No. Feeling okay was beyond her. She was terrified to go outside and falling for a guy who wasn't falling for her. Not permanently, anyway. She wetted her lips. It had been a very long day. Most of it spent waiting for him. She concentrated on the circles under his eyes. Knew they mirrored her own.

Dusk flooded her living room, and it suited her purpose. Enough thinking. Enough brooding. She lifted her hands and undid the top button of her dainty summer blouse.

"I was waiting for you."

He tossed a file folder onto the coffee table and slowly came to stand in front of her. Every muscle worked in conjunction, a sinewy grace causing his clothes to pull and stretch in all the right places. She followed the centerline of his body up until she was looking at his face. She paused.

He held out a hand.

She accepted. "How about a little something to take the edge off?"

"I thought you wanted to talk?"

"Pillow Talk."

"Guys don't do pillow talk." He tucked a curl behind her ears, a whisper of a touch, and it gave him away. He didn't realize it, but she did. "But I might be convinced to make an exception for you."

"I can be very persuasive."

"Or is that stubborn?" He put an arm behind her

knees, the other around her shoulders, picking her up like she weighed nothing. He bent his head and brushed his lips against hers. "You deserve better than me."

She laid a finger against his lips. "That's for me to decide."

He trapped her finger between his teeth and swirled his tongue around the tip. His scent floated around her, drugging her. She loved the way he smelled, and her eyes did a slow roll back behind closed lids. It made her neck yearn to stretch and expose the tender, erogenous zone behind her ear. It tightened the internal cord connecting her brain to her vagina and snapped it tight.

"I missed you." She tugged her finger out of its trap and pulled his head down toward her. She was going to savor every second with him, every inch of him.

Under the sheets, there were no dark circles, no tender hearts, no past history. The intensity shifted to fulfillment and connection, zoning out by making love.

Later, she found him sitting on the living room couch hunched over a file folder, clad in only jeans and his Saint Thomas of Aquinas medal. She pulled the edges of her sweater closer together and leaned against the wall. The coward in her decided the future could wait one more night.

"How's the investigation going?"

He looked up, ran a hand through his hair. "Not good." He dropped the file folder on the coffee table.

"Anything I can help with? You know, in a non-threatening, wrapped-in-cotton kind of way." He studied her for a minute, long enough to have her squirming and pushing away from the wall.

"Actually, you might be able to help with this." He motioned her over to sit beside him.

"Okay." Hope blossomed and held her captive.

"These are the tips we've received in the last few days. The word is out and people are trying to be helpful." He picked up the file. "We need to weed out the crazies and the ones that have no direct relation to our case."

The folder was surprisingly thick. One glance at the top message had her looking back at Chase. "This one's from Mrs. Ruttan." Her eyebrows went up. "Her dog hears things?"

"I've pretty much ruled that one out. Maybe you can go through these and pick out the ones that might be helpful?"

"Sure."

"I'll make coffee."

"Sounds good."

"All right." He headed for the kitchen as she jumped on the hope roller coaster.

The edges of the file folder curled under her fingers. She set it down and smoothed it out then opened it up. Determined to find something they could use to stop the madness, she did a quick flip through the pages. People were looking to help and reporting anything and everything.

She flipped back to the beginning and got to work. By the time Chase came back with the coffee, she had a couple with potential set aside.

"Anything?"

"Maybe." The mug of coffee was warm in her hands, soothing almost, and she took a fortifying sip. "These might be promising."

Chase gulped down a quick mouthful before setting the mug down. "Okay. Which ones?"

"There you go." She watched as he bent his head, and her heart lurched. She focused on the pile of notes, frantic for a diversion. "The top one is from Mrs. Curtis. I doubt very much she'd call unless she had a good reason."

"It's regarding her neighbor's property. Mrs.

Lewis is still around?"

She laughed. "You bet. Her grandson, Mason, is in my class. In fact, he and Jason are pretty tight." She leaned against Chase, trying to get a look at the message. "I'm pretty sure Mrs. Lewis is out of town, visiting her youngest daughter. She's expecting a baby any day now. You probably remember Crystal?"

"It's says Mrs. Curtis swears someone's been in Mrs. Lewis's backyard while she's been gone. Several times. Trampling her friend's garden."

"Very strange."

"Mrs. Curtis." He frowned. "So, Mrs. Lewis is away? You're sure?"

She lifted a shoulder. "Pretty much a hundred percent. And likely, Mrs. Curtis would be the one keeping an eye on things."

"Something's not right. I think I'll go check it out. I'll get Mike to meet me there."

"Wait a minute." She set the folder down and got to her feet. "Meet us where?"

"Mrs. Lewis's. And it's meet 'me' there. As in, me alone."

"I'm coming."

"No."

"I promise I won't get in the way." She wrapped her arms around her stomach to keep the contents from lurching around. It was dark out, and the last thing she wanted was to be alone. "I've been cooped up here all day. You don't know the address. She moved about three years ago. I promise I'll be good. I need to go with you."

His eyes flashed. "I swear, if you so much as put your little toe outside of my truck…"

She crossed her heart. "I know the drill. I'll stay put."

He sighed and pulled her in close. "I'm not going to let anything happen to you, I promise."

She pressed in closer. "I believe you."

He stepped back to let her pass, only to wrap those long strong fingers around her arm and halt her in mid step. "I promise he's not going to get to you. Or Jason. Not ever again."

"I know." She did. She knew it. He was her Superman, but even Superman had his kryptonite.

The ride took less than five minutes. She tried to act passé about the whole endeavor, but she was too busy trying to ignore the dark and its host of shadows.

"What's the number?"

She squinted harder into the dark and did a quick study of the street. "I'm not sure of the street number. Oh, there. That one right there. With the cute fence and the pretty little chairs and table on the front porch."

He muttered something that sounded like "fuck sake," but she ignored him.

She frowned as they drove past. "Where are you going?"

"Round back, down the alley." He cruised down the alley and parked outside the appropriate gate about halfway down. Out came his cell phone. She listened as he explained things to Mike, then watched him stuff the phone back in his pocket before reaching past her to open the glove compartment and grab a flashlight.

"I won't be long."

"I'll be waiting."

He yanked open the truck door, got out, and paused to stare at her. A look flitted over his face a second before he leaned back in. "Come here."

And she went because she wanted to, because she needed to, because it was Chase. He tasted of sanctuary—strong, safe and familiar. He pulled away and she sighed at the loss. She clicked the locks shut as Chase disappeared through Mrs. Lewis's back alley gate.

To distract herself, she did a quick survey of the cab of his truck. She tapped at the air freshener hanging from the rearview mirror. The glove compartment caught her attention, made her wonder what else he kept in there. She sucked in her top lip and reached a hand out. Bad idea. Worse, it smacked of desperation.

She leaned against the passenger door, rested an aching, tired elbow on the armrest. The headlights shadowed the mixture of tall grass and heat-resistant weeds lining the fence. Further down the fence and into the dark, there was nothing, not even a breath of wind to wave the odd tired bush. Everything was waiting—the plants, the air, the dirt, and her.

She scanned the ground, blinked into the darkness, and did a double take back to the area of the fence three feet to the left of the truck. She leaned forward to get a closer look and clunked her head on the window.

She grimaced as she massaged the sore spot. It looked like a backpack. In fact, she was sure it was a backpack half hidden by a bush. Even with only the headlights of the truck to go by, she was positive. She knew her backpacks. She had one hand on the door handle before she remembered the dark and what it hid.

She looked around, made a half-hearted attempt to knock on the windshield. She blew out a breath. It was resting right there against the fence. Of a very dark and empty alley, and even with Chase fifteen feet away, it scared her to be alone out there.

She dug through her purse for her phone and dialed Chase. "I think I found a clue."

"You found a clue? Sitting in the truck?"

"Yes, it's right there. Against the fence. A backpack."

"Why are you whispering? Are you sure you're in

the truck?"

"Yes, I'm in the truck." She'd said she'd be in the truck, hadn't she? Although, in all fairness, she'd promised to stay put before and hadn't.

"Okay, I'll be right out. Whatever you do, don't leave the vehicle."

"Right." She glanced down the alley as she listened to him say something to someone. Mike must have parked in the front of the house. As she watched out the window, a figure rounded the corner of the alley and paused, took a couple of steps in, and paused again. She pressed the phone tighter to her ear. "Um, Chase?"

"Don't worry, I'll be right there."

"There's someone at the end of the alley."

"What?"

She ducked down to the floorboards and hissed, "Someone's at the end of the alley, just standing there."

"Get down and stay down." The order echoed in her ear. "Lily?"

She hated not being able to see what was going on. "I'm already down."

She waited. And crammed twenty-four hours of anxiety into five seconds. The light tap jolted her eyes to the side window, and she squinted up at Chase before scrambling to unlock the doors.

"There's no one there now."

"But I saw someone. Standing right down there." She pointed in the direction of the streetlight at the end of the alley.

"I believe you, and someone's gone to check out the area. So, anything specific you can tell me? A description of any kind?"

"Okay, good." She swallowed before pushing her hair back and concentrating. "Not that tall, maybe five ten. Definitely under six feet. Dark clothes, jacket, but the hood was up, and it's dark so I didn't see much. Slight build, not buff. Sorry that's it."

"No, that's good. And where's the backpack?"

"It's right over there." She pointed at the fence.

"Mike?" He glanced behind him and pointed.

"I'm on it."

"Are you okay here for a while longer?"

She nodded.

"I won't be long." He dug around behind the seat and pulled out a beat-up leather jacket and handed it to her. "In case you need it."

She shrugged into it as he walked back through the gate. She rubbed her cheek against the leather before reaching over and turning the radio on low enough for her to hear the soft music, but not loud enough to cover up outside noises. He might not remember, but she did. All the times she'd sat huddled inside his coat at some outdoor bush party, or parked down some lane or dirt track. She'd always given it back at the end of the night, despite protests. She'd known he only owned one coat.

The scent of leather and faint whiffs of aftershave made this jacket smell the same. It made her feel safe, protected. Her eyes drooped, and she blinked back the drowsiness while snuggling deeper. She remembered everything. Every little detail.

****

Chase sighed and waited for Mike to radio the situation into the detachment. The backpack needed to be handled with extreme care. Who knew what it contained? What it hid? Who it belonged to? Chase didn't believe it was dangerous, but there was protocol to follow. And it wasn't the only thing they'd found. Someone was using the tiny shed to hide away. A spot, well hidden, that didn't attract attention, because the owner was out of town.

He thought of the blue bandana bagged as evidence. Hopefully the blood on it would tell them something. Otherwise, there wasn't much in the way of solid proof. Discarded chocolate bar wrappers weren't going to tell them much. Pointless to ask who knew Mrs. Lewis would be out of town. The entire town probably knew the occupant of 46 Elm Street was awaiting the arrival of her newest grandbaby. The question was how a member of the Prairie Brotherhood knew, and why they'd bother with it.

"It's too far from Lily's to be any help to the Brotherhood." Chase rubbed a hand over his rough jaw, his brain slogging through the facts.

And who'd been in the alley? Not Tessier. Not according to Lily's description. Tessier was over six feet and about two hundred pounds. Once again, more questions than answers.

Mike set the camera down and picked up his flashlight and pointed it at the back of the shed. "Exactly. Why would one of the Brotherhood hole up here when they had a place out of town? It doesn't make sense."

"We're missing something." Chase picked his way around the side of the shed, his own flashlight in hand, and then to the front again. "What's the connection between an elderly widow and the Brotherhood?"

Mike swung his light along the fence. "None that I can think of."

"Is there any connection between Mrs. Lewis and Jason?"

"They're probably aware of each other's existence."

Something was nagging at the back of his brain, but Chase couldn't quite put his finger on it. "They'd be able to keep tabs on Jason easier from here. Stay close, but not too close."

"It's a possibility," Mike said. Beams of light continued to crisscross the large, lush backyard; over the birdfeeders, garden gnomes, ripe vegetable garden, and rust-colored shed. "It's what? Two blocks to the McCarran's? Less if you cut across a few yards."

"Damn it. Something's not right. I just can't put my finger on it." Mind cloudy with fatigue, Chase struggled to shift through his conversations from the last twenty-four hours.

Mike rested a hand on his shoulder. "Look, we're all running on fumes. Why don't you take Lily home? We'll finish up here and let you know what happens with the backpack."

"I'm going to take you up on that offer." He hadn't heard Lily, but he was getting ear strain listening for her. He pressed the button to illuminate his watch. "Then I'm catching a couple of hours of sleep. Your shift's long over, you should do the same."

Mike scrubbed a hand over his face. "Yeah, as soon as we're finished up here."

"Let someone else do it. You look like hell. Get some sleep."

Mike slapped him on the shoulder. "Thanks, buddy."

And then Chase had it. The connection. Between Mrs. Lewis and Jason. He put a hand up to stop Mike's departure. "Shit. No one from the Prairie Brotherhood is holing up here. Before we came, Lily mentioned Mrs. Lewis's grandson and Jason are good friends. Son of a bitch, Kevin McCarran's been hiding out here all this time, right around the fucking corner. We need to sweep this place. What if what we're looking for is right under our nose? We need to get the backpack back to the detachment and examine every inch of it."

Chase headed for his truck, adrenalin pumping energy into muscles too tired to do anything but twitch in response, and opened the door. Even with the interior light on, she didn't budge from her spot slumped against the passenger door. He hopped into the truck and shut the door with a soft click. The motor rumbled to life, and Lily's lids didn't flicker. His temporary buzz dissolved.

Pale, bruised, and exhausted.

Up to her pretty neck in terror and hanging on by pure grit and stubbornness. He admired that, admired her. The leather of the steering wheel protested under his cold hands. Admiration? *At least be honest.* It didn't have a damn thing to do with admiration.

His.

Every pore of his skin knew it. His heart beat to the truth of it. His brain screamed it. The knowledge licked at his soul.

She slept. All that separated them was a cup holder, twelve inches of upholstery, and ten years' worth of denial and personal conviction. He felt a rot-gut twist of panic.

He had a career he loved. Thrived on. He'd landed exactly where he'd planned, on top of his game and a specialist in his field. He'd run from exactly one thing his entire life——a five-foot-four-inch, red headed girl. His Achilles' heel. God help him if Raphael Tessier ever found out what Lily Marie Wheeler meant to him. She broke the bank as far as bargaining chips went.

And he wanted her. That life. That fairy tale. But not enough to endanger her life. Not enough to be her family. Or give her one.

No. It ended after this was done.

He parked in her driveway. One glance at her proved she hadn't moved the entire ride home. Next, he scanned the front of the house. Hard to tell anything in the dark. But nothing set his spidey-sense tingling. Keeping his eyes open for trouble, he headed for her front door, unlocked it, and disabled the alarm. So far, so good. He made short work of getting her out of his truck, hoping some of his heat would keep her warm. There was a definite chill in the air tonight. A signal summer was ending.

She stirred in his arms and he whispered, "Shh. You're home. Go back to sleep."

"Home?"

"Yup."

"Good." She rested her forehead against the nape of his neck.

"Now go back to sleep."

"Come, too?"

"I'll be back later. Don't worry."

She perked up. "Did you find something?"

"We're not sure. Possibly. I'll let you know later, when I get back. Right now I'm going to tuck you in."

"Okay." Her eyes drifted shut. "I miss you."

"I'm not gone yet."

"Just wanted you to know."

His soul sighed. It had to end soon. He needed some distance. Before he forgot the vows he'd made to himself.

Chapter Thirteen

The squeal of tires torching the pavement pushed Chase out of Lily's bed at five o'clock in the morning, after a grand total of five hours sleep. He stuffed his legs into his jeans, ripped open the drawer of the nightstand, and grabbed his 9mm pistol. On the move, he stuffed his cell phone into the front of his pants.

"What is it? What's going on?" Lily struggled to sit up and clutched the sheet to her.

"Probably nothing." But saying it didn't make him believe it. He grabbed the ammunition cartridge off the nightstand and pushed it into the handle of the pistol. "Stay here."

He was halfway down the hall in the time it took to grasp the slide of his gun and push it back.

"Wait a minute."

He ignored Lily's shout of protest from the bedroom. It was the rustling that came next he didn't dare tune out.

"Stay put until I check it out." Still more movement, and he growled to get her undivided attention, "Get down and stay down."

The sound of peeling rubber propelled him in the direction of the front door. Through the small glass panel to the side, he caught sight of a sedan speeding away. He flicked on the outside light. Inched the door open. The second he noticed the lump on the grass, he placed a call to nine-one-one.

On high alert, he opened the screen door and stepped out onto the front steps. The early morning chill puckered his skin. He ignored it and concentrated on the body. As his feet left the cold concrete and sunk into the damp early morning grass, he squinted through the darkness.

No movement. He zeroed in, definitely human. Hunkering down beside the body didn't make identification any easier in the dim predawn light. Two fingers pressed next to the victim's windpipe told him what he already knew.

Dead.

The knife sticking out of his chest spoke to cause of death. He pushed a hand through his hair. And because dead bodies never became routine, he swallowed back the reaction of his rolling stomach.

Son of a bitch, what was next? He scanned the lifeless street again. Why? Why bother? Why risk getting caught? Unless they knew? Unless they were watching? But from where?

His focus sharpened as he rotated in a circle on the grass. Lots of angles. But not many possibilities. The clock ticked on, time running out. For Tessier, too. Chase searched past the row of rooftops lining both sides of the street. Nothing for the naked eye to see.

He jumped onto the tiny porch and headed back inside to check on Lily. She was dressed and perched on the edge of the bed. A short prayer for her protection came and went. In the end, he trusted his experience, the men and women who had his back, the weapon in his hand.

He explained as best he could while tossing on more clothes. Left the room with strict instructions for her to stay put. Sirens sounded in the distance. Chase scanned the street before leaving the safety of the house and was out the door as the lights flashed around the corner. Vehicles screeched to a halt.

Doors swung open as police officers and rescue personnel clamored out. Lights came on in windows up and down the street. Front doors opened as a few brave souls ventured out. An officer made quick work of motioning them back. Another young officer strode toward him, looking a little green around the edges.

Chase could sympathize. Instead he said, "Late model four door sedan. Dark in color. Too dark to see the license plates. At least two people, driver plus one passenger. Headed north and turned right at the corner."

"Got any idea as to his identity?" The officer jerked a thumb in the direction of the body.

"We can start by checking for a tattoo on the inside of his wrist. A triangle dissected by a stalk of wheat, in blue ink."

They approached the body and the surrounding circle of professionals. The officer hunkered down beside the body and reached out a gloved hand to lift the wrist. "Hard to tell, the area's pretty mutilated."

"Mutilated, how?"

The officer winced. "I think it's been removed."

Chase stared at him, and the officer gave a slight incline of the head.

"And there's a note."

"A note? Let's see it."

"It's currently being held in place by the knife."

Chase closed his eyes. "Shit. Is it legible?"

"I don't know. But that's not all." The young officer swiped a hand over his mouth. "He's missing his hands."

"Okay, first things first. Let's take a look at this note." He knelt beside the body. "Shine your light closer here, will you?" The first rays of dawn began to brighten the sky. But it wasn't enough to enable them to make out what was written on the bloody piece of paper stapled to the guy's chest with the blade of a bowie knife.

Blood had soaked into the scrap of white paper, making the markings all but illegible. However, a man didn't need a shitload of brainpower to decipher the word NEXT printed in big black letters. Someone handed him gloves, and he snapped them on.

"Can I borrow your light?" He held out his hand. The light traced a path of horror from the tip of the victim's head to his bloody shoes. "They beat the shit out of him first."

"Looks like. Coroner is on her way."

"I'd bet six bucks and my left nut we've found the Prairie Brotherhood's cook we scared up on our little search of that farm yesterday."

"He didn't get far."

"They never do." He stripped off the gloves and stood.

****

Lily stared out the window, hands around what had once been a steaming cup of coffee. There was a dead man on her lawn. This ride on the shock and terror roller coaster was getting old. She wanted off. Thank goodness Jason and his aunt were safe. Not even she knew their out-of-town location. Only his social worker and the police had access to that information. One more layer of security. One more way to keep him safe.

What did these people want? What could be so important? Worth a human life?

Outside her window, they lifted the body bag and put it on the stretcher. She shuddered. Chase stood in conference with Mike, his stance wide as if braced for more worst-case scenarios, the two of them discussing and gesturing. She swigged back more cold coffee.

The hiccup of breath caught her by surprise. An urgent need to sit dropped her onto her couch, her forehead hit her open palms as the air thickened and clogged her throat. The couch dipped, and she swayed with the movement. She hadn't heard him come in, but she was glad he was here now. All she wanted was his warmth, and strong arms around her. Her anchor in the storm.

"Hey, Lilypad." He pulled her close and she went, not because she was weak, but because she was smart enough to know where she needed to be.

She gulped out a laugh. "There's a dead person on my lawn."

"I know."

"I'm going to be fine. I just needed a little time." The long strokes up and down her back soothed and surprised her.

"Okay."

"Who is he?"

"We don't know yet. Likely one of the Brotherhood."

Gritty with fatigue, her eyes drifted shut. "Why would they…you know, it doesn't even matter. Whoever he was, he didn't deserve to die like that, no matter how he lived his life."

"Your capacity for caring for the wrong sort scares the shit out of me."

"There is no wrong sort."

"See what I mean."

She elbowed him in the side.

"And we still have to deal with his gang banger brothers."

"I know."

Her coffee mug ended up in his hand, and before she could stop him, he swallowed. She waited until he finished coughing before explaining. "I added a little something to the coffee."

"A whole lot of something." He pounded his chest.

"I'm calling it staying power."

"How much staying power have you had?"

"Just a cup." She trailed a finger across his jaw, over the shadow of stubble, made note of the dark circles, sallow skin, his weary eyes. "You're exhausted."

"I'll be fine." No answering smile. He caught her finger in his hand. Never one for huge ear-to-ear smiles, even his quirky, slow grins were appearing less and less often.

Her front door opened, and Mike called out before wandering into the room. "Okay, I think we're good to go."

"Meaning no more dead guy on my lawn?" She patted the seat beside her. "Come join us. Have some coffee."

Mike glanced sideways at Chase and raised his eyebrows.

"Don't ask. And don't drink the coffee."

Mike grimaced. "Ah. Too bad, I could use some...coffee right about now. Just letting you know I'm on my way back to the station."

"I'll be right behind you."

Lily rubbed her eyes and sighed. Back to work. It had to end soon, this tension and fear. Normal. She craved normal. And remembering brought her back to last night. She grabbed Chase's arm. "Last night? Did you find out anything?"

"Nothing useful." He patted her hand, a very bad sign. "But we're getting closer. Don't worry."

Don't worry. Right. She would just hit her don't worry button. Or drink more coffee. Anything to keep from dissolving into a clinging mass of insane.

****

It was virtually impossible to scrub blood off grass. No magic moisture-absorbing towel existed capable of exorcising that kind of stain, or the accompanying twelve-times the horror, so she settled on scouring the kitchen floor the old-fashioned way, down on her knees. It was either that or skip further down the insanity trail.

Rumor had it manual labor helped a person think and she needed all the help she could get. She was beyond exhausted. Her body, every muscle, gasped for relief and answers. It left her feeling like a Picasso painting—put together all wrong.

As the forty-eight hour deadline loomed, fear for the safety of her colleagues and students kept her sequestered at home. Too much time and not enough. The disposable cell phone Raphael Tessier had given her sat silent, like a live hand grenade on her kitchen countertop. Her watchdog of the hour, Stan Knight, paced her living room, his own phone glued to his ear. She wasn't quite sure what his presence meant in the grand scheme of things, but she was going to find out.

And her own personal Superman was doing who knew what.

She wished him back. Because she missed him. The man. She wanted to blame it on some type of untreatable sexual addiction. But she was becoming more addicted to the nonsexual touching. The hug from him this morning, the way he liked to tuck her hair behind her ear, and intrinsic gentleness he refused to acknowledge. She wanted so much to love him. If only he'd let her.

She sank down onto her knees and dumped the brush into her bucket of suds. Displaced bubbles bobbed around her. At some point, she was going to have to tell him how she felt. To ignore it, disguise it, trap it, were cowardly options, and she was not a coward. Telling him, acknowledging her feelings, before he left was the right thing to do. The adult thing to do.

She yanked out the brush and started scrubbing. The bristles scraped across the floor, back and forth in manic swirls. A patch of hair slipped from her messy ponytail, obscuring her vision.

There'd been a dead person on her lawn, and she was worried about her love life. She stuffed the strand of stray hair back into place. Selfish. Selfish. Selfish.

The floor glistened as she dipped the brush in the water and slapped it back across the tiles again and again. Chase was going to get himself killed protecting her. And wasn't that a crushing thought. She dunked the brush back in the water and whacked the floor again. Not knowing what to do, how to fix it, waiting for answers was taking its toll.

Water flew everywhere. Bubbles settled in her hair, on her nose, on hot cheeks. The scent of lemons burst into the air. Poor Stan rushed into the kitchen and stared at her, clearly afraid she'd lost it.

Laughter filled the tiny kitchen, too much loon in it to be healthy. But it beat the alternative hands down, even if Stan appeared skeptical. She sobered up when her phone rang, not the evil one but her landline. She couldn't not answer it. She'd tried. The worried, concerned messages left by friends and neighbors persuaded her to start answering again. People were also leaving bits of information, ninety-nine-point-nine percent useless, but good intentions were good intentions and she obliged them by listening. She'd dubbed it Lily's Hotline.

Stan nodded and even though she didn't need his permission to answer her own phone, she felt better, reassured.

"Hello?" A fit of coughing had her frowning and wary. The sudden silence set her nerves on edge. "Hello? Who is this?"

"Listen to me, little girl." She pulled the receiver a couple of inches away from her ear, but not before she recognized the slosh of liquid against the inside of a bottle. "I'm sick to death of your interferin' in my boys' lives."

"Mr. McCarran? Are you drunk?" The very idea

incensed her, pulled something ugly up from her gut she didn't know was hidden there.

"Screw you, little miss teacher." Another swig of liquid going down. "You don't know nothin.'"

Her patience burst along with the last of her soap bubbles. *Stupid, stupid, old man.* Her hand tightened on the receiver, but she refused to be drawn in by a lowlife like Jake McCarran. "This conversation is over."

"You'll never find him, you know."

She hesitated, risked a glance at Stan who was frowning at her. He held out his hand, offering to take the call for her, but she shook her head, anger burbling up around the hate and cracking her fragile composure. "If you've had contact with Jason—if you've endangered his life in any way I swear..."

She gritted her teeth at the peal of liquid laughter and the ensuing coughing fit that interrupted her tirade.

"I'll get him back. Ain't no one can stop me."

"I'm stopping you." She was going to make it her life's work to stop him.

"You need to understand somethin' lady. That's my blood you're messin' with." He backed the statement up with another wheeze.

"I know exactly who I'm messing with." The fact that he was anyone's parent sickened her.

"That include the Brotherhood? Because I promise they'll bring the wrath of Satan down on your little head, missy. Just like they did my boy."

"Jason is safe and will stay that way as long as you leave him be." And what was she thinking trying to rationalize with the irrational?

"Jason? Maybe. But it's almost too late for my Kevin."

"Kevin? What about Kevin?" She gripped the counter as her heart started to pound in high alert. "Do you know where he is?"

Another swallow and more sniffles. "Never you mind. He's safe. God's protecting him now, and you'll never find him."

Her gut clenched. If she could manage to get him to tell her something, anything that would help them put an end to the madness, it would be worth showing some patience, some sympathy. "What's Kevin got to do with this, Mr. McCarran? What do you mean God's protecting him?" Her hand shook as she signaled Stan to start writing her words down.

"Nothin.' Ain't none of it his fault."

"I'm sure it's not, but maybe I can help him." Her sole goal centered on keeping him talking, she saturated her words with as much sympathy as she could stomach, until he gave her more, something to work with, something to guide her.

"That gang banger's got his balls in a vice. And for nothin.' He don't have what they're lookin' for." He was yelling now.

"Tell me." She closed her eyes and took a deep, silent breath. "Tell me why he feels he's in trouble, and I can help him."

"You!" She cringed as he sucked mucus back into his nasal passages. "You and that cop will do him as much harm as the Brotherhood."

"No, I promise you. We won't—"

"You already did. We had it all under control until you interfered."

"What under control? Please." *Please, more information*. Keep him talking. Begging seemed like a small price to pay.

"No one will ever think to look where I hid him. No one. Everyone but God's forgot that place now."

Her front door opened then shut, startling her, and she bobbled the phone. She managed to catch it at waist level and bring it back.

"You aren't getting another one of mine."

"Mr. McCarran, please—"

She brought the phone down to stare at it, the dial tone echoing into the air. She glanced up to the sight of Chase halted in the kitchen doorway.

"That was Jason's dad, Mr. McCarran." She shook her head to help clear the rattling. The idea stuck with her. "I think he might have accidentally told me where Kevin's hiding."

Chase scrubbed at the back of his neck as Stan exited the room, or maybe escaped was a better word, mumbling about a fact he had to check out. Lily waited for him to say something.

"You're like some freaky trouble magnet."

"I can't believe these things keep happening either." Her forehead wrinkled. "But this is a good something. Right? If we can find Kevin, we can find what they're looking for."

"Where exactly do you think he is?"

"Safe Harbour Bible Camp."

"Is that a joke?"

"No." She clamped a hand on his arm in emphasis. "He said Kevin was somewhere safe. Protected by God. Someplace everyone's forgotten."

"I think you've been reading too many Dan Brown novels."

She squeezed his arm. "I'm serious. He's out there. I know it."

"I hate to burst your junior detective bubble, but we've got every reason to think he's in town."

"Why? What did you find out?" Her mind raced, and she went back to last night. "The shed! You think that's who was hiding in the shed."

"Lily—"

She let go of his arm and paced out her thoughts. "The man in the alley? It was Kevin! He must have run to his Dad, and his Dad took him out to the old Bible camp." She spread her hands out and smiled. "That's it, isn't it?"

Chase sighed. "We don't know that for sure. But

I'll go check out the Bible camp idea."

"You're not even going to consider a request to take me with you, are you?"

The telltale muscle in his jaw twitched. "I won't be gone long." He moved closer and stroked her cheek with his thumb. "I promise."

Her hands slid up his chest. "Be safe."

"Always."

"Good." Her hands slipped into his hair and brought his head down until his lips were a lick away. She whispered, "Because I love you."

Because she was watching, waiting for it, she saw his eyes age sixty years in six seconds. "You don't know what you're saying."

"I know exactly what I'm saying." The exact thing he didn't want to hear. She held on tight, her heart under mortar attack, and waited for his denouncement. It didn't take long.

"I'll call you after I get back." Her hands ended up in his, and he offered a quick squeeze before making his way to the door. No lingering kiss or prolonged touch.

"I don't expect you to say it back." Time gave a person ample time to think. She'd had the whole morning, before the floor scrubbing incident, to plan, to decide on a course of action. His pause and rigid body stance told her all she needed to know. His hesitation gave her a couple of seconds of preparation before he faced her again.

She smiled, but it drooped at the corners. "You don't have to say anything. Take what I said with you. Test it out, see how it feels."

Wrap it around you and let it keep you safe.

His nod did nothing to reassure her. His exit, even less. She wrapped her arms around her midsection in an effort to hold everything together. She'd said what she had to say. She bolted the door, set the alarm, and sat down to wait him out.

Chapter Fourteen

The road was rutted and cracked and deserted. And if it weren't so flipping cheesy, Chase would have added, like his heart, except it wasn't so much cracked as shattered. All the king's men and all the king's horses couldn't put it back together again, or some such crap and bullshit.

He concentrated on the freakin' trees. Tall alternating with short, they edged right up to the road. Trees and more trees. He was losing sight of the big picture. The steering wheel jerked in his hands as yet another hole in the road tried to swallow a tire.

I love you.

Forget it. Forget her.

Hadn't he tried? Hadn't he given it his best shot? And he was still right back where he'd started.

Add to that, he was out in the middle of nowhere looking for a place near water everyone but God had forgotten. On the say so of some drunken, broken down old man who didn't give a shit about anything except where his next drink was coming from, and a small town teacher with a Nancy Drew complex.

I love you.

As if. She didn't know what she was talking about. Finally, a sign post. He slowed the truck down and leaned over to read the sign. Safe Harbour Bible Camp and Retreat, Next Right. There was a smaller Closed for the Season sign tacked sideways over top. Closed for the season? More like closed for the last decade. He wasn't making any more stupid comparisons either, like same as his heart.

Because that would be pathetic.

He drove a couple of feet further, stopped, and peered down the overgrown dirt track. Half a mile in, Chase gritted his teeth as branches screeched over the hood of his vehicle and whipped their way along the sides of his brand new truck.

I love you.

Shit. Like he didn't know it. Like the knowledge wasn't crawling under his skin looking for a place to nest, searching for a home. And damned if he didn't want to give it one. Too tempting. Too everything.

He cranked his truck around a ninety-degree turn only to slam on the brakes once he rounded the corner, the gunshot blast snatching his attention back. The sight of the old man in the middle of the path aiming his rifle at him had him unlocking the glove compartment and reaching for his own weapon. He stuffed it into the back of his pants, forcing his head back in the game.

He lowered the driver's side window. "Lower you weapon." He opened the driver side door and slid out to stand behind the door. "Now."

"You got no business here. Move along." The wrinkled old gnome gestured with the gun and puffed out his skinny flannelled chest.

"I'm a member of the Aspen Lake RCMP detachment. Put the gun down, now." *You idiot.*

"Where's your car, your uniform, or your badge? Show me some proof."

"I've got my badge right here." Okay, not so dumb. He palmed his credentials and put both hands in the air.

"Come closer so I can see it."

"Not until you point the gun at the ground."

The crazy old coot lowered the gun, and Chase

took a cautious step out from behind the door.

With a neutral expression and never taking his eyes off the gun toting hillbilly, he inched closer, showing Beavis his badge and hoping Butthead wasn't hiding in the bushes.

The gun jerked in the old man hands.

Chase stood his ground.

The old man squinted at him. "Step closer."

The man leaned forward, then swung the gun to his shoulder, his finger still resting against the trigger. "About time you showed up."

The whole place was crazier then he remembered. He stuffed his badge in his back pocket. He slid his right hand over the gun resting in the waistband of his jeans. "Sir, lower the gun and put it on the ground."

"No need. I know what I'm doing."

"Sir, do it now." His fingers curled around the handle.

"No need to get antsy." The old man put up a hand.

"Now." He kept his eyes wide open and focused straight ahead. "And by that I mean immediately." He wanted that line clearly drawn in the dirt. Plain and simple. "Do it now."

The old man's eyes narrowed. "No need to get surly."

His finger slipped off the trigger. He seemed surprised when Chase yanked the gun from his gnarled twisted grip.

"Hey, gimme back my rifle."

"No." He made a quick job of removing the cartridges. "Is it registered?"

"I don't need no damn registration. And I've got no use for a government that says I do."

Chase ignored him. "What did you mean when you said it was about time we showed up?" And it better not have anything to do with UFO landings or escaped livestock.

"Someone's been using the old camp." He leaned in, whispered, "Hiding out."

"You've seen this person?"

"Took a shot at him, in fact." He nodded his white-haired head up and down all over, pleased with himself.

It was probably too much to hope he'd shot Tessier.

"Shame I missed, too. The eyes aren't what they used to be. I'll be sure to get closer next time. Harder to miss at close range."

Okay, Gramps was getting his gun back over his dead body.

"Can you show me where this person's been hiding?"

"Sure can."

"You the owner of this property?"

"Yes, I am. Abraham Dawson, but folks call me Ham." Guaranteed if he'd had suspenders he would have snapped them, instead, he held out a steady hand.

He accepted the offer. "Constable Chase Porter, if I could have a look around, I'd sure appreciate it."

The old guy rocked up onto his tiptoes and back onto his heels, glee spreading across his wizened face.

"Are you freely inviting me onto the property?"

"Well, I guess I am." The invitation, freely given, made things a whole lot less complicated.

An hour later, he was no closer to an answer than he'd been yesterday. No Kevin McCarran. No great big neon sign saying Prairie Brotherhood goons this way. Nothing except more garbage, similar to the stuff in the shed, and Ham the Hillbilly.

He kicked at a couple of plastic containers lying on the floor of the abandoned bunkhouse, stopped beside an old sleeping bag, and inspected the drug paraphernalia. If Raphael Tessier didn't kill Kevin McCarran first, his drug habit was going to do it for him.

He bent down to study a piece of scrap paper when his ears caught the clunk of boots on the rotting floorboards. A shadow flashed across the doorway, and then a body appeared. One glimpse at Chase, and the body was on the run.

"Stop. Police." He was on his feet and out the door of the bunkhouse.

The body sprinted toward some bushes covering the left corner of the building.

So not going to happen, buddy.

"Police. Stop." He was not losing this guy again.

The assailant stumbled at the unexpected sight of Ham rounding the corner, but righted himself in time to grab onto the old man.

The knife appeared out of nowhere. One skinny arm wrapped around Ham's wrinkled neck. Kevin McCarran's arm shuddered and the ripple effect followed a path to his hand. Chase's gun was in his hand and pointed at the target. He welcomed the rational thinking, encouraged the instincts that came with it. Relished the state of knowing what to do. "Let him go."

"Or what, you'll shoot me?" The sneer and sweat running down the sides of his face and soaking his shirt were at odds with each other. Misplaced confidence and desperation curled up together under a drug addict's pale skin.

"Let's all calm down." Chase didn't care for the look in the old man's eyes. Worried he was plotting something stupid, he issued a warning. "Ham, do not move."

Ham ignored him, intent on valor. "I think you should shoot him. Take out his knee caps first." The knife pressed a little harder against his throat, and

Ham had the good sense to squirm.

"Shut up, old man." Kevin dragged Ham back a couple of steps.

"I heard shattered kneecaps hurt like a son-of-a-bitch." Ham might be up there in years, but he was feisty.

"Ham." Again, Chase put as much shut-the-fuck-up as he could into it.

Steady, with every muscle straining under his skin, he willed the old man to keep still. The hand holding the knife continued to shake. Kevin McCarran was surprisingly strong for someone who was stoned and weighed all of one hundred and forty pounds soaking wet.

"Let's all calm down."

"Back up!"

"Put the knife down."

"Do you think I'm stupid?"

"Boy, you're so damn ignorant you couldn't find sand if you fell off a camel." Ham jabbed a bent finger in Chase's direction. "Just shoot him. He deserves it."

Chase gritted his teeth and ignored the old man. "Kevin, I don't think you're stupid. I want you to understand that I'm not the enemy. The Brotherhood is. I can help you." He moved an inch closer.

"Man, are you delusional? The only thing that can help me is to help the Brotherhood and give back want they want."

"Tell me what they want, and I can help you." Forward another inch.

"The whole fucking point is to keep the thing out of the cops' hands."

A very bad feeling slithered up from Chase's gut. "What are you talking about?"

"The last person I'd give it up to is a cop."

"Give what up?" Another inch.

"You think I'd tell you?"

"I can help you."

Kevin laughed and backed up a step, dragging Ham with him.

"You can trust me." Chase was close enough now to make out the scabs and scratches on his arm, like Kevin had tried to scratch his way out of his own skin.

"You think Raphael Tessier will let me live if I give it to you? You're stupider than you look."

"Why is Raphael Tessier interested in what you have?"

"Evidence."

"Evidence? What evidence?"

"Like something the cops would love to get their hands on."

"That covers a lot of ground." They were running out of time. "Be specific. You're in a position to help yourself, Kevin. Tell me what I want to know and we can work something out."

"Make a deal with the cops?" He spat a wad of spit into the dirt.

"It beats being dead. Think about it, Kevin." Chase had one card he hadn't played. He hoped Kevin McCarran had enough of a soul left to spare a thought for his little brother. "And while you're at it, think about Jason. Tessier is after him. Your little brother. And sooner or later he's going to find him. Do you want that on your conscience?"

"No." Kevin squeezed his eyes shut. "I never meant for that to happen."

"Okay. Then let's figure out how to fix it. Start by letting Ham go."

"I can't." The trembling wasn't going away. It was getting worse. Kevin stumbled back a step taking Ham along. Chase was running out of options. So was Kevin. It showed in his efforts to tighten his hold on the old man. "You can't put me anywhere the Brotherhood won't find me. Tessier's going to make me pay. And pay. And pay."

His agitation escalated. He shook his head like a dog shaking off water. Ham was stronger than he looked, and smarter. He stomped on Kevin's instep with his boot heel, and then slammed his elbow into his stomach. Kevin doubled over, knife in hand.

"Kevin, drop the knife."

Kevin dropped to his knees, his cheeks wet with tears, the knife dangling from his fingers.

"Kevin let me help you." Chase motioned for Ham to get behind him, relieved when he obeyed.

"Help me?" The knife dropped to the ground. Kevin lifted his eyes, and then shifted them to the gun in Chase's hand. His eyes begged Chase to act, and he followed it up with a tap on his forehead. "Being dead is the only thing that's going to save me. Please."

"I'd said I'd help, and I will." One cautious step at time, Chase moved toward the knife and picked it up. "But only you can help Jason. He's your true blood brother. The only one you've got. And he's in big trouble."

Spent, Kevin hung his head. "A gun."

"What's special about this particular gun?"

"This one has Tessier's fingerprints all over it."

"Probably plenty of guns out there with his prints on them."

"Not a gun he used to shoot a cop."

"What?" Chase narrowed his eyes. The world tipped on its axis. The air hardened. His stomach heaved, and his finger tightened on the trigger. "Which cop? Explain how it came to be in your possession."

Kevin McCarran lifted his head. "I'm done talking to you."

****

Lily rolled the good luck pebble she'd found in third grade back and forth between her palms. She hated waiting. Too bad her life was one big wait and see. Action, she needed action. As a last resort, she looked to the piles of marking awaiting her attention—essays, homework assignments, quizzes. And as a last, last resort she could continue to fidget and dwell on the Deadline of Death.

It was a toss-up. Stewing required less effort, but in the end she settled on productive. She grabbed her huge tote off the hallway table, stopped in the kitchen to let Stan know where she'd be, and headed to her office. At least, she gave it her best effort, but the task of focusing eluded her. Concentrating proved impossible.

She'd said the "L" word. Out loud. She refused to take it back. She didn't want to. It was honest, heartfelt—ill-timed, but genuine. She slid open her desk drawer and pulled out the little ornamental box she'd shoved all the way to the back. Caught up in the past, she traced a gentle finger over the filigree markings. The delicate clasp opened with barely a touch.

The image of Chase telling Jason about the picture of his Mom he'd kept hidden from his father came and grabbed hold. There'd been no one to hide this picture from except herself. She picked up the locket, the broken chain slipping through her fingers, and flipped it open. There they were, frozen in time, laughing and carefree. He'd been gone a week before she'd yanked it off and thrown it out of sight. Like a bad penny, or a golden thread to the past, it always made an appearance when she moved or rearranged. When she'd rented this house, she'd stashed the necklace in the little box, unable to throw it away.

The locket disappeared into her closing fist. She lowered her head, shut her eyes, and willed him not to do anything stupid. The same applied to her. Be calm. Don't panic. Hope for the best, prepare for the worst, and in the meantime, be productive.

She grimaced at the pile of marking in front of her. They were studying Romeo and Juliet and she'd asked them each to write an alternate ending to the play. She picked up the top paper. A feather touch of something in her mind gave her pause, but it slipped away before she could grasp it. It was either let it go or drive herself crazy. Despite the paper's poor construction, it provided a much needed laugh.

Again, something tickled at her subconscious. Pushing her chair back, she frowned as she settled back and reached for the speck of something in the back of her mind. But the stack of papers made her think of Jason and she rubbed her arms. Thank goodness he was out of harm's way.

Then it clicked. The little something niggling at her. She gave her forehead a smack. She might as well get it out of the way. Digging around in her tote for his file, she set it aside. That's what was twigging at her. Jason's homework. She'd forgotten all about it.

She dug through her neat piles. Pulling out Jason's work, she added it to the work she collected from his other classes. She was left with a half-finished math assignment, a social studies paper, and the essay. She picked up the math sheet. It was a miracle he'd finished even part of the assignment with the pressure he'd been under.

Next she picked up his essay assignment and frowned. The weight of the paper was wrong. Something was glued between the pages. Her brows drew together. She flipped the page over and stared at the back. A tiny SD card was taped to the paper. Flipping to the front, she stared at the words. She picked up his math assignment and glanced over the answers to the questions. The answers appeared to be the same ten numbers written over and over again.

SD card?

Groups of numbers?

She laid the paper down and with a gentle hand, smoothed it out. The combination to something? It had to be a combination to a lock. She couldn't image he'd have the combination to a lot of locks. His school locker, maybe a locker at the local rec center, something locked up in his house. But why give her the combination if it wasn't for his school locker? She dug her fingertips into her temples and rotated them. It must be his locker. Had to be for his locker.

She retrieved Stan, hustled him into her minuscule office, and all but shoved him into her office chair.

"Right there. See?" She forgot to let him answer as she stabbed at the numbers. "The numbers. It's for a combination lock. It has to be."

Stan opened his mouth. She noticed, but excitement kept her talking. "Jason sent me a message. And more importantly, he gave me this." She wagged the paper with the tiny SD card still attached to it in Stan's face.

"Careful, don't—"

"I don't know what's on it, but it's got to be important. Right? Maybe lead us to whatever it is that Tessier wants?"

"That's for the police to decide."

"Well, then let's hand it over to the police." If they could wrap things up before her forty-eight hours were up, better for her. Better for Chase. Better for them all.

****

"I'll do it." Lily sat perched on her couch, trying to stem the thrill of excitement over being involved in the big take-down as she thought of the plan.

"There are serious risks involved. You need to

take longer than three seconds to think it over." Chase radiated displeasure, it permeated the air. The need to touch overwhelmed her, and she reached out. Big mistake. He bolted off the couch.

"Is this what's got you twisted up in knots?"

"I'm serious." He pointed a finger at her, which should have made her furious, but only made her sigh.

"I know that." Seriously, she got it. He'd been at it since he'd slipped in her back door and sent Stan out the front. "But the risks are worth it if we can be done with Raphael Tessier for good."

"I still don't like it. There are other ways."

"Or there's this way."

The little disposable cell phone rang. Lily stared at it. Out of the corner of her eye, she saw Chase stiffen. The ring sounded again. She glanced at him. He nodded his agreement. She picked up the phone.

"Hello." She hated that her voice wobbled and her hand shook. Hated that Raphael Tessier scared her sick. He was early. Wasn't he early? The forty-eight hours weren't up yet.

"Eleven p.m. tonight. The Danforth place." The line went dead.

She set the phone down. Her little drizzle of excitement fizzled. Game on. One with no rules and no assurances. No guaranteed outcome.

****

"You do not make a move without my say so." He hated this. Hated it.

"Scouts honor. No improvising of any kind."

Their forty-eight hours were up. They had to give RT something. They had a plan. Play on their advantage and use the odds turning in their favor for the first time in a very long time.

While Kevin McCarran crawled up the walls of his temporary cell, other officers opened Jason's locker and secured the gun he'd hidden at the back.

Chase had watched the scene on the SD card and relived the horror of the alley in all its gruesome glory, his part in it.

More than anything, he wanted to put what had happened there behind him, wanted to honor a fallen colleague and damn good friend by apprehending his murderer. The son of a bitch was going down. But every best option had a worst-case scenario written in the fine print. His frightmare put Lily front and center and, if things went wrong, into Raphael Tessier's hands.

"I don't like it," he repeated for what had to be the tenth time.

Lily sighed. "I know. But this isn't your decision. It's mine."

For the trap to work, they needed Tessier and the Prairie Brotherhood to believe the police had left Lily under-protected. She needed to play a part. That it had come to that was killing him.

"Okay." He turned to address the assembled group. "We're banking on the Prairie Brotherhood being oblivious to this afternoon's events." They'd kept things as quiet as possible and on a strictly need-to-know basis, but it worried him.

"Don't worry. It'll be fine," she said. He glanced at her, so calm. Confident things would work out. She almost had him believing it was true.

Right. Because what could possibly go wrong when a small town teacher is offered up as bait like an appetizer fly to one of the country's deadliest spiders.

"But we're not taking any chances." Not this time. Not with Lily. "We're also banking on Tessier assuming Lily will tell me everything. Plan on it. So, we'll go over it once more. We split up. Some of us at the old farmhouse, that's the prearranged meeting spot, in case some of his people show. But he's got something else in mind. He's got somewhere else to hide, to watch from. Somewhere close. My gut tells me he's going to come at her from there."

The tricky part was betting on what direction his Plan B would take. Stan had yet to check in. Chase was counting on him coming up with something big in terms of Raphael's possible secret location.

"Reinforcements from a neighboring detachment were handling the abandoned farm and meth lab site. Mike will stay with Lily." Chase needed to be seen leaving Lily, to have Tessier believe he'd managed to outsmart the police. Only then would Tessier let his guard down.

Chase's cell phone rang, and he yanked it out of his pocket. "Tell me you've got it."

"Was there ever any doubt."

"He's in place?"

"Just arrived."

"Where's he watching from?"

"You're never going to believe it."

Chapter Fifteen

It was time to move. Chase was getting ready to head out. Low voices drifted around her, going over calculations, then double checking and triple checking. Chase was leaving first to make it look like he was heading for the meeting site. Then he would double back. Mike stayed with her. And they'd wait for Tessier to show his hand. They knew he was watching her house. Thanks to Stan Knight, they also knew from where. She tucked her sweater in tighter around the protective vest they'd given her to wear. She watched, fascinated by the interaction, by the background thrum of excitement, by the attention to detail. She winced as Chase slapped a hand on Mike's shoulder and grinned. He came over, hunkered down in front of her.

"Ready?" His expression steadied her nerves—confident, calm, reassuring.

She dipped her head. "Ready."

He took one of her hands in his. "This is all going to be over soon, and life's going to go back to normal. I promise."

That was the only part of the plan she didn't look forward to, but knew was inevitable.

"Chase?" They both glanced in the direction of the hall and the rest of the group. Chase gave her hand a squeeze and stood up. Her fist clenched around the disappearing warmth of his.

Lily looked up at Chase. "I'll be here waiting."

She tried for a laugh, but didn't quite pull it off.

Chase didn't smile. Instead, he looked behind him. "Mike."

"I'm here." He walked up to stand beside Chase and grinned at her. "Looks like it's you and me, beautiful."

"Take good care of her."

"You bet." Mike winked at her. Chase shook his head in disgust. Lily let a small smile slip.

"Okay, I'm off." He smiled at her. She held her breath, suddenly not wanting him to go. Offering up a prayer for his safety, she smiled back. "Stay safe."

"Always." As he headed for the door, she folded her hands in her lap. This was it. Soon it would be over. Jason would have his life back. Things would return to normal. Except she didn't want her normal back. She wanted Chase. A chance at forever.

****

They waited for the phone to ring. When it did, Lily reached for it with an almost steady hand.

Mike put a hand over hers. "Remember, you need to keep him talking, to distract him. It's not going to take Chase long to double back, the rest of his team is ready to move. I'm right here. There's no way Tessier can get to you." She nodded and picked it up.

"Hello."

"Did you think you could out maneuver me, little teacher?"

"I'm guessing that's a rhetorical question?" She tried to bank the revulsion, to move past it, to quell the volcanic sized urge to throw up.

"Here's what you're going to do. You're going to walk out your door. Alone. Phone in hand, and you're going to follow all of my instructions. Leave whoever's babysitting you inside."

"Why should I do that?"

"Because I said so."

"That doesn't work for me anymore." But it did, the threats worked her over and hung on.

"Oh, it will. Because, otherwise, I'm going to grab the first person I come across and butcher them into little pieces. You might be surprised at who I find, because I'm closer than you think. That little boy that lives across the street from you? He's cute isn't he? What's his name? Levi."

Lily felt the blood drain out of her head, the sweat pop out onto her skin. Mike motioned for her to keep talking but she couldn't...

"Lost for words, little teacher?"

"You're despicable." Distract him. That was her job. Keep him talking. Focused on her. Buy some time.

Raphael Tessier laughed, and the hatred gurgled up out of him. "I was born on the street. I've lived my whole life there. You don't know despicable from shit."

"I know you killed your girlfriend." She swallowed past the nausea. "Did she get in your way? Did your unborn child deserve to die with her?"

"Shut your mouth. Just shut the fuck up. You don't know anything about it."

"Judge, jury, and executioner. Even if they're blood. Or innocent. Or good and kind and everything you're not."

"Get your ass out the door. Now."

"No."

"You're my get-out-of-jail free card. I'm not letting you go. You're mine."

"No. I'm. Not."

"Either you come out, or I'll tell Levi you said hi."

Chase, where are you?

Mike mouthed the word, "Okay?" She jerked her head. Then she heard a commotion in the background. Voices shouting.

"You bitch. You're dead. Do you hear me? Dead." The heated threat rang in her ears. More shouts sounded, muffled this time. Tessier's voice, Chase's commands.

Then they came...the sweetest words she'd ever heard sounded in her ear before the line went dead. "We've got him."

****

"On the ground, hands behind your head. Do it now." Chase pressed the gun against Raphael Tessier's temple, and tossed the phone. He slipped his handcuffs out of their place as officers swarmed the tiny bungalow across the street from Lily's. The one with the SUV and the little boy. The house where Raphael Tessier, aka Lawrence Dalton, had worked a brief stint as a construction laborer. The house he entered from the back alley. The house he'd copped a key from and used to let himself in and out during the day and some nights, depending on the family's schedule, which was posted on the fridge in organized, convenient detail, including their weekend away.

Raphael Tessier squirmed under his hold. Not as detached as he wanted everyone to believe.

"Your fellow *brothers* are outside face down in the dirt."

"Yeah, doesn't mean we're done. Not you and I. Not my Brothers."

"Get him out of here." Chase hauled Tessier to his feet and signaled to a fellow officer. Before he forgot who he was and the oaths he'd taken.

"We're not so different, you and me." Tessier smirked "We each protect our own. Hold ourselves to certain standards. Do what it takes to get the job done. And my job's not done."

"We've got the gun, we've got the video. And for the record, we're nothing alike." Chase didn't need Raphael Tessier to plant that seed. It had been planted years ago. His enemy didn't need to know it.

"It was supposed to be you in that alley." Tessier's eyes were as dead as ever. Nothing showed there, no remorse, no panic, no humanity.

"But it wasn't. So now it's my job to make sure you pay for what you did. If it takes me the rest of my life."

"You're a dead man, Porter."

"How original. No criminal's ever said that to me before." He grabbed Tessier's wrists and shoved him at the door.

Tessier twisted and tried to break free.

Chase didn't so much as blink. "Don't give me a reason."

"You don't have the guts. Just like your partner."

"It wouldn't take guts to shoot you. It doesn't take guts to be you, in case you're wondering what we're all thinking. It did, however, take guts to be that thirteen-year-old kid. But you know what? Keep it coming. We love it when the bad guys volunteer a confession." He motioned to the cop coming up behind Tessier as he began citing the Canadian Charter warning.

Chapter Sixteen

Too jittery to stay home alone, Lily waited on a chair in the police station for Chase. She needed to see him with her own two eyes. Needed to run her hands over him. Needed to know he was safe.

The clock on the wall pointed to well past midnight. She clasped the disposable coffee cup tighter between hands still suffering from the odd convulsive jerk. The sight of a friend crossing the floor toward her had her jumping out of her seat, desperate for the distraction.

"Here let me help you." Lily reached out her hands for the baby while his mother struggled with an overflowing bag.

"Lily! What are you doing here? Is everything okay?"

"It's fine. I'm waiting for someone. How's the little guy?"

"Fussing and refusing to sleep, so we went for a ride in the car and to see daddy. He's supposed to be on break so we decided to drop by."

"Are you here to see Daddy?" She cooed as she propped the baby against her shoulder and rubbed his back. She pressed her face against his soft hair and inhaled his sweet baby scent, the refreshing smell of innocence, such a nice change from the horror of the last few days. She let his silent baby music lull her into a gentle sway. Out of the corner of her eye, she caught sight of Chase stopped four feet away. In one piece. Safe. A little grim around the edges but, hey, who could blame him. It had been a harrowing few days.

"Hey, there." She smiled and kissed the baby's head. "Ready to go?"

He cleared his throat. "Yep, ready to go."

She turned, her arms full of baby, and motioned to the woman next to her. "This is Danielle Weins. Jeff's wife." She settled the baby in the crook of her arm. "And this is Evan." She grinned up at Chase.

"Nice to meet you, Danielle." He motioned to the baby. "And Evan."

"Nice to meet you, too." Danielle smiled. "And welcome back to Aspen Lake."

"Thanks." He nodded to Lily. "You ready to go?"

"Sure." She couldn't stop the tiny frown. Something was wrong. Wasn't he supposed to be happy, relieved, thrilled to see her? She handed the baby off to his mother with a promise to get together soon.

She sprinted to keep up with him, his long strides leaving her lagging a couple of paces behind, all the way to his truck.

She grabbed his arm to slow him down. "Is everything all right?"

"It's fine." He shrugged her off, opened the truck door and helped her inside.

She settled back against the seat, still frowning. Waited while he rounded the truck and climbed in beside her. He stared straight ahead. Her insides clenched. "Are you sure? Because you're not acting like it is. Raphael Tessier is locked up, right?"

"Everything is fine. He's not going anywhere anytime soon."

"Are you going to tell me what's on the SD card?"

"No." A muscle in his jaw jumped. Fair enough. It wasn't any of her business anyway.

"I think you need to tell me what's wrong."

"You looked good holding that baby." Was that a good thing or a bad thing? She wasn't sure.

"Um, thanks. I think." She glanced at his hands wrapped around the wheel, back to his side profile, eyes straight ahead, watching the road as he drove. Studied the stiff, closed body language and the grim expression. "You're sure everything's fine?"

"It's as fine as it's going to get."

Well, that didn't sound promising.

"What's that supposed to mean?"

He never took his eyes off the road. "We'll talk about it when we get home."

She liked the sound of "when we get home." She reached out to touch him. It hurt worse than she would admit when his whole body tensed up. She let her hand slip down into the space separating them. Silence filled the cab of the truck and lasted throughout the ride to her house. She waited until they were inside, the alarm set, before she reached for him.

"I'm so glad you're okay."

"Lily—"

They'd deal with everything else in the morning. It could wait. Tonight was for celebrating, for rejoicing, for putting the light back in his eyes.

Her lips explored his neck and nibbled their way along his jaw line to his ear. And because she was desperate, she imagined his eyes drifting closed. Imagined his arms ungluing from his sides and wrapping around her. Imagined he loved her back.

"Make love to me." Her hands went to work on his shoulders, his neck, and his control. She used precious seconds to find the pulse point on his neck and suctioned it into her mouth. Rasped her tongue over it. Then kissed her way back to his ear. "Slowly. Over and over again."

Wanton thoughts. Dark images flooded her

brain. Her hands gravitated to his waistband and deep down in the tightest, darkest places, her body rejoiced at the feel of his erection. She softened, stretched, contracted, and pushed aside her heart's whispered misgivings.

The hiss of his descending zipper egged her on. She battled for eye contact. Forced the word she needed to hear across his lips, her hand sliding into his jeans, stopping to circle and pulse around him. She fought to win. To keep.

"Yes." Hoarse, grainy, and ripped from him.

She laid her lips over his and whispered it back to him.

****

Chase couldn't close his eyes without seeing her holding that baby in her arms. His worst nightmare and his greatest longing. His reasons for resisting infected with hope. He pressed against her hand, wanting her to clench harder, to pump faster.

Blind, deaf, and on fire.

He lifted her up. Carried her through to the bedroom and to bed. He let her slip down, until she was standing in front of him, before the bed, and he took a mental step back.

"Strip it off." Her blue eyes flashed, widened. He smiled, even though his heart wept. "I want to watch you strip down. I want it to go slow. I want you to think of my mouth on you, my fingers inside you, and my cock dripping for you as you do it. I want it to take forever." Because the memory of it needed to last him a lifetime.

Light, he needed the light, and reached over and switched on the bedside lamp. He memorized as she stripped, stretched, and arched toward him, bent away from him, and back again. Relished the deep blue of her eyes, caught the little intake of breath as he slipped his T-shirt up and off. Made sure her eyes were on him as he shed the rest of his clothes.

On his knees in front of her, he placed his hands on her stomach and laid his lips against her womb. His eyes closed and this time, the little intake of breath was his. He imagined the stomach under his hands rounding, growing with child. His child.

Madness.

His fingers spread to her back absorbing the warmth of her skin. He pressed closer taking in her scent. Her fingers trickled through his hair, scraped across his shoulders as his hands tracked the curves of her backside, danced down the back of her legs, spreading them wider with each stroke. His lips worshipped, explored, and ventured lower while her hands clamped onto his hair, her nails raking over his scalp until they stopped, dug in and held on.

His mouth and tongue and teeth worked her over until her legs started to shake and panting breaths filled the air, his and hers. When her body buckled he guided her back onto the bed and flipped her onto her stomach. He traced the lines of her back while her hands dug into the covers and gathered them in, he nipped at each and every one of her twenty-four vertebrae, he kissed the dip at its base and gloried as her back arched. He pushed his hands along her back and up into her hair. His mouth followed and nipped at the back of her neck, her muscles tightening under the stroke of his tongue, her legs parting wider with every lick, nip, and kiss.

He wanted more. So much more. On the brink. Which way to go? More.

Face to face, he mapped a memory of sensitive breasts, puckered nipples, her curved belly, and the jut of her hipbones. His shoulder blades curved and arched under the bite of her nails.

"Look at me," he urged. Knees and heels slid across sheets to make space for eager hands. "Look."

With his lips on hers, his eyes looking into hers, his arms spreading her wide open, he said goodbye.

Once she was asleep he reached back and switched off the lamp. In the dark, he started the whole process over again. His hand ran over her hip and down her leg as far as he could reach. Back up and down her arm and on to her hand, the tips of his fingers memorizing the feel of her limbs, the curve of her stomach, the weight of her breasts. His face turned into her hair clinging to the pillow beside him. The silky softness carried her scent to his soul. He willed his brain to remember how she tasted.

He kissed a shoulder blade. The mole he knew to be two inches to the left. He wanted to pull her closer. Stay forever. He wrestled his resolve back into place. She deserved a real family, and he couldn't give her one. He didn't have it in him.

He pulled the covers up, tucked them in around her, and slipped off the bed. He made it as far as the bathroom, stumbled in, closed the door, and leaned back against it.

He couldn't breathe.

Hands on head, holding everything in. Not working.

Couldn't catch his breath.

His legs started to shake, and then his knees buckled. His back slid down the cold wood of the door. His ass hit the unforgiving floor, his knees came up, and his head fell forward.

His woman.

His family.

His eyes locked shut. He grabbed fistfuls of hair to stop his head from slamming back against the wood of the closed door.

Not his.

Not now.

Not ever.

Chapter Seventeen

She listened to him leave the room, waited while he finished up in the bathroom, and willed him back. She was shocked when it worked. The kiss was light. The whispered, "We'll talk in the morning," filled her with dread. She pretended to sleep, listened to him dress, and thirty seconds later, the front door opened and closed.

She pulled his pillow closer and clutched it to her. Inhaled the scent of sex, of man, of pleasure. Something was wrong. Something she wasn't sure she could reach, or fix, even if she could. Something so ingrained, so wrapped in layers of history and tied up tight with misplaced intent, it was important only to him. She wanted to dig up his dead father and shoot him full of holes, hack off body parts.

She tried calm thoughts. Tried to get back to sleep. Gave up. Checked her bedside clock. Two in the morning. She sighed and bided her time.

At four o'clock, she showered, dressed, and sat down to wait. At six o'clock, she walked over to Chase's and knocked on his door. No one answered. His truck was there. He couldn't be far away. She sat down to wait. She'd wait forever if she had to.

He ran up the walk, his hair standing up in wet spikes, and stopped dead at the sight of her.

"Hi there," she offered in way of greeting.

"What are you doing up so early?" He avoided eye contact, choosing instead to turn and watch a car drive down the street. Lily's heart lurched.

"Not sleeping. Same as you." She wanted him to smile, to look at her, to make a connection.

It wasn't going to happen. He grabbed the front of his shirt and mopped his face and neck with it. She stood and smoothed a hand over her jeans. The silence was deafening.

"So, are you going to invite me in?" she asked.

"Yeah, sure. Of course."

He led the way to the kitchen and the coffee pot. "I'll put some on, then go and clean up. You'll wait?"

"Go, shower. I'll put the coffee on."

She knew what she wanted to say. No doubt he was rehearsing his part in the shower. She lifted the cup to her lips and sipped. Set it back down when he came around the corner and stopped to lean against the doorframe, leaving space between them, his gaze going past her.

"Lily."

"Don't." She shut her eyes, blocking out the set line of his mouth, the carefully flat eyes, the crossed arms.

But she couldn't close her eyes forever, and when she opened them, he was staring directly at her.

"The last thing I want to do is hurt you."

Her heart stuttered at what she saw in his eyes. She lifted her chin and met his gaze head on. "Then don't."

He turned his head and stared at the dark waiting outside the window.

"This isn't easy for me, either." His gaze swung back, warrior fierce and focused on her. "I can't give you what you want."

"What is it you think I so desperately want?"

"A life. A family. Stability. A husband who'll be home every night. I can't..."

"Have you ever asked me what I want?"

"No, but I—"

"No, you haven't. No more than you took my wants and considerations into account ten years ago."

"Oh, come on, I saw you last night, holding that baby."

"So, I held a baby. I'll even admit I enjoyed it." She sucked in a deep breath. "But babies are not the one thing I can't live without." *You idiot.*

"You say that now, but what about in two years, five years, ten years? Are you going to feel the same way? How about when you're moving with me around the country?"

"I guess you'll never know."

"You don't think I'm dying here, Lily? I'm trying to do the honorable thing, and it's killing me."

"Killing you?"

"Lil—"

"And you still don't get it." She frowned and spread her hands out in a question. "Those decisions are mine."

"Your life is here. It's all you ever wanted. Don't deny it."

"Maybe I will deny it."

"And yet here you are—a teacher, in the same town you grew up in. You're rooted here like the damn aspens this place is named after. You've found your anchor here. I find you putting your life on the line for some kid. So pardon me if I don't quite believe you." The look he sent her was hardened by determination. "I won't be the one to take it all away."

She put her hands on her hips. "And last night. In bed. What was that about?" She'd been enthralled. He'd been…

And it dawned. The light came on. She took a couple of steps forward and jabbed a finger into his chest hard enough to send him back a step. "Last night was about goodbye for you, wasn't it, you coward?"

He raised his hands in the air to deflect another jab. She watched his jaw jump even as his teeth clenched.

She jabbed him in the chest again. Instead of a step back, this time he grabbed her hand.

"Careful."

She invaded his space and pushed him back another step with both hands. "Or what?"

He closed his eyes. "Don't push me, Lily."

"Or you'll what?"

He opened his eyes and stared at her.

"You can't even say it." Her breath hitched on the last two words. She paused, seeking composure. Her teeth bit into her bottom lip until she tasted blood.

"Just because I can hold it together today, doesn't mean it won't happen tomorrow."

"That's plain stupid. You've been so busy nailing yourself to a cross you don't even realize you're giving up a life that has happily-ever-after written all over it, complete with our own ending."

"What alternative ending? You tell me what that would be."

"Here's a wild thought. Maybe all we'd need is each other. Maybe our family could consist of you and me. We decide how the story goes. You and I. Destiny doesn't care about sickness or health, it doesn't acknowledge for better or for worse, it doesn't make love, have fights, communicate, go on holidays, or do the dishes. Destiny doesn't live every day, day in day out, with anything. People do. We make our own choices. Destiny is possibility. Life is work."

"Stop it."

"No. You stop it." She swiped at her hair. "You're the one hung up on the idea of children. On some ridiculous notion you'll end up like your father. You're nothing like your father. Your dad never held it together a day in his life. You're worried about me and how I'll deal with your job? Thanks for the vote of confidence."

"I'm doing what's best for you." His voice rose, and he took a step back.

"You're doing what's best for *you*." The decibel level surprised even her. She inhaled a couple of deep breaths.

"You weren't there. You don't know."

"No, I don't, you never gave me the chance."

"You saw me that day on your deck. Is that a man to love?"

"I'm standing here, aren't I?" She put a hand on his arm to stop him from turning away. "I'm standing right here. Right now. Hoping for forever." She put her hand over his heart.

"I'm sorry. I'm not willing to bet on forever."

"Then I guess you've gotten what you always wanted." The fight drained out of her. There was too much history, too much backstory that time could not erase. "You're alone. And I'm done waiting for you to realize you're giving up the best thing that's ever happened to you."

She grabbed the medal that hung at his neck and tugged. "You wear her protection and guidance around your neck, but it's like she never existed even for the short time she was with you. Her memory deserves better. I deserve better. If you're going to leave, you need to get it done and leave."

Her exit was a thing of beauty. Pride got her through the front door and then deserted her. She fought her way inside her own house and out to her back deck, waited for the sun to rise, wishing the day was over. Unfortunately, an exit was counterproductive to her initial goal. The chill cycling through her veins spread a throbbing, muscle-deep sadness through her whole body. She was too cold to cry, too tired to move, and too drained to care.

He'd wanted a memory. She'd wanted forever.

Fool me once, shame on you. Fool me twice, shame on me. Shame on her for believing in second chances. For building that white picket fence around him a second time. How many times did he need to bulldoze it down before she came to her senses?

She did deserve better, but she wanted better with him.

****

In the end, it took Chase twenty-three hours, forty-seven minutes, seventeen miles, two hundred and seven sit-ups, half a bottle of Jack Daniels, plus a visit to his mother's grave to realize he couldn't live without Lily. One decade and a handful of days to realize he didn't have to try.

He owed her an explanation. An apology. The truth. And the rest of his miserable life, if she'd have it.

He'd left her alone for the rest of the weekend. He'd watched her go to work on Monday morning. It was now Monday night, and he was hesitating on her doorstep like a teenager on his first date. He patted his back pocket, then pushed the doorbell.

The door opened, a good sign. She didn't slam it shut at the sight of him, which was an even better sign. The need to reach out and touch had him locking his knees in place.

"Can I come in? Please?" He willed the door open further.

She frowned, but stepped back. "Sure, come in." She led him back to the kitchen where she stopped and waited.

"I thought about what you said the other day and I wanted to explain."

She held up a hand. "I think we've said all that

needs to be said on that subject." She turned and leaned against the counter and wrapped her arms around her stomach. Protection. From him. And it hurt more than he could say.

"I wanted to explain why I left." He shoved his hands in his front pockets. "The first time."

"It doesn't matter anymore, Chase."

His fingers clenched. "It matters to me."

She shrugged. "Excuse me if I'm no longer interested in what matters to you."

He pushed on anyway. "Ten years ago, up until five-fifteen on June twenty-eighth, being with you was the only thing that mattered to me."

"Chase."

"Let me finish. Please." He pushed a hand through his hair. "Then my father stumbled home, demanded I give him money, and took a swing at me when I refused to hand any over." He shook his head. "It was the final straw in a long list of…shit."

He stopped to take a look out the patio doors and collect himself. "My plans changed after I pounded in his face, after I'd washed his blood off my hands, after I dropped him off at the Emergency Room. It was my worst nightmare come true, being like him. Something he threw in my face every chance he got. What's bred in the bone.

"I couldn't stand it. I couldn't risk doing the same thing or worse to you." He held up his hand when she looked about to say something. "You think that's stupid, I get that. But I was eighteen years old. I'd already been in love with you for two years. It felt like an obsession. It felt like everything my father used to tell my mother. How he couldn't live without her, how they'd always be together, no matter what happened. I needed the last ten years to learn how to be a man, the right sort of man. To prove I had something positive to offer. To prove it to myself."

“I know you don’t want to hear this, but I’m going to say it anyway. I’m so sorry for the things you had to go through as a child. I’m so sorry you had to make your way all by yourself. And I’m even beginning to understand your reasons for pushing me away. But that’s the past. What about today?”

She dipped her head, but not in time to hide the sheen of tears. When she looked at him again, all trace of tears had disappeared. He wasn’t sure if that was a good or bad omen.

A gust blew in the open screen door of the patio and lifted her hair and tossed it over one cheek. He started to reach out to tuck it back, but she beat him to it.

“I’ve got something for you to see.” He swiped his sweaty palms over the thighs of his faded blue jeans before reaching into his back pocket and pulling out a bunch of folded papers. “Look them over and see what you think.”

“Okay.” She took the papers, opened them, and started to read. He relished the tiny wrinkles of confusion marring her pretty forehead. She looked up. “You bought the house next door?”

“As a sign of good faith. As a sign that I’m staying, right here, in this town, next to you. And if you don’t want to leave when the job demands I go, you’ll have the place you always wanted.”

“Why?” Hope was turning her voice soft.

“Because, even if it takes the rest of my life, I’m going to prove I’m the man who deserves you. Deserves you forever. And if you’ll give me a chance, I’ll try to explain it better over dinner or maybe the rest of our lives.”

She bit her bottom lip. “We’ll figure out our next move together?”

He stepped closer, opened his mouth, shut it, and then opened it again. He placed one hand on her cheek, and then the other one. The rub of his finger over her bottom lip had her closing her eyes.

"I love you, Lily. I've never said that to another woman, never even thought it."

She opened her eyes and lifted her chin. "And you think that will erase all our problems?"

"No. But if you give me a chance, we can work on them. Together. A lot of things about this still scare the shit out of me. But I'm willing to work on why."

Her lips curved. His heart lifted.

"You were right the other day. You are literally the best thing that's ever happened to me."

She smiled. "You're right. I am."

He bent his head and laid his lips across hers in a soft caress. "I love you. There's no getting rid of me now."

She ran a hand over his cheek and slid it back into his hair. "I love you. Always and forever."

He tugged on her hand. "Come on, there's something I want to show you."

"What? There's more? This must be my day for miracles."

He twined his fingers through hers and led her all the way to his backyard.

"You wanted to show me a bunch of boards?" He almost laughed at the disappointment spreading across her face.

"A special bunch of boards. To be painted white and put up together, in a row, to make a fence." He swept an arm all the way around the yard. "A white picket fence. Our white picket fence."

"Do we know how to build a white picket fence?"

"What we don't know, we'll figure out as we go."

She launched herself at him, and he caught her. She wrapped her legs tight around him and squeezed.

"Do we know how to build a dog house, too?"

"I'm sure we could figure it out. Marry me, Lily."

She squealed and squirmed and kissed him on the mouth.

"Is that a yes?"

"Yes. Yes. Yes."

With one hand in her hair and one arm holding her up, he moved toward the back door. "It's good to be home."

A word about the author...

Karyn Good lives in the Canadian Prairies with her husband and two children surrounded by blue sky and wheat fields. When she isn't writing or herding children, she's hiding in a corner reading.

www.ingramcontent.com/pod-product-compliance
Lightning Source LLC
Chambersburg PA
CBHW072224170626
46813CB00003B/1081